This Is the Wizard's Secret Weapon

1 The Dawn Swordsman

relatively mature adult to a student who is still an immature and developing youth! And we've gone from a story with a strong nuance of self-discovery to one of love and adventure among young people who are heading full speed ahead in pursuit of their future dreams! This work depicts a story that I wasn't able to include in *Bastard Magic Instructor*! But of course, I'm sure it's a story that fans of *Bastard Magic Instructor* will also enjoy!

I hope you will all look forward to seeing where I will take this new story as a writer!

Also, I post updates on X (formerly Twitter), and I'd be very happy if you would DM me or reply to my posts and send me messages of support or other thoughts about my works. It really encourages me and brings my motivation to the max! My username is @Taro_hituji.

That's all for now! See you in the next volume!

Taro Hitsuji

Afterword

Hello, Taro Hitsuji here.

I'm pleased to bring you the first volume of my new work, *This Is the Wizard's Secret Weapon*!

I would like to express my infinite gratitude to the editors and publishers, as well as the readers who have picked up this book. Thank you very much!

Now, that aside...

How should I put this...? Readers who have been following my works since the recently completed *Akashic Records of Bastard Magic Instructor* must surely be saying something like...

"That damn Hitsuji... He wrote *another* magic academy story?!"

And, well, you're absolutely right! Guilty as charged.

After so many years of writing a story about a magic academy, this new work is yet another magic academy story?!

I know! I'm well aware! I'm even thinking the same thing!

But! If you read it, you'll see! You should understand—while this new work, *This Is the Wizard's Secret Weapon*, is set in a magic academy like *Akashic Records of Bastard Magic Instructor*, the two works read completely differently from each other!

As for the protagonists, we've gone from an instructor who was a

"At this rate...
you will be expelled."

"Brother...
If you don't
return to the
Mercenary
Corps, there'll
be nothin' but
death in store
for you!"

"Whaaat?! Why
is my future
such a mess?!"

The next volume
is coming soon...

This
Is the
Wizard's
Secret
Weapon

1

The
Dawn
Swordsman

INDEX

This Is the Wizard's Secret Weapon

This Is the Wizard's Secret Weapon

1

The Dawn Swordsman

Taro Hitsuji

Illustration by
Kurone Mishima

YEN
ON

New York

This Is the WIZARD'S Secret Weapon 1

Taro Hitsuji

Translation by
Genevieve Hill-Kaminishi

Cover art by
Kurone Mishima

KORE GA MAHOTSUKAI NO KIRIFUDA Vol. 1 REIMEI NO KENSHI
©Taro Hitsuji, Kurone Mishima 2023
First published in Japan in 2023 by KADOKAWA CORPORATION, Tokyo.
English translation rights arranged with KADOKAWA CORPORATION, Tokyo,
through TUTTLE-MORI AGENCY, INC., Tokyo.

Yen On
150 West 30th Street, 6th Floor
New York, NY 10001

Visit us at yenpress.com · facebook.com/yenpress ·
twitter.com/yenpress · yenpress.tumblr.com · instagram.com/yenpress

First Yen On Edition: June 2025
Edited by Yen On Editorial: Rachel Mimms
Designed by Yen Press Design: Andy Swist

Yen On is an imprint of Yen Press, LLC.
The Yen On name and logo are trademarks of Yen Press, LLC.

Library of Congress Cataloging-in-Publication Data is available.

ISBNs: 979-8-8554-0869-0 (paperback)
979-8-8554-0870-6 (ebook)

$PrintCode

LSC-C

Printed in the United States of America

Prologue

Why I, a Mercenary, Decided
to Become a Wizard

"All right! I managed to successfully die in battle...! Now I'm freeeeeeeeeeeee!"

In the ruins of a battlefield in Bertrandt, in the eastern reaches of the Ford Continent...a boy with dark hair and eyes—Rix Frestat—cried out in joy.

He was in his mid-teens, slightly taller than average, and had a fairly toned physique covered with old scars.

From his unwavering stance, the tattered leather armor covering his body, and the one-handed sword hanging at his hip, one could tell he wasn't just some innocent youth.

And he wasn't. This boy, Rix, was a mercenary.

He was an ace attacker in the Black Mercenary Corps, the most powerful and infamous fighting group in the Eastern Conflict Zone.

"I've gotta say...that was quite the realistic performance I put on back there."

Rix thought back on what he had just accomplished.

That's right—he had been "killed in action."

Rix had taken up the rear guard to help his mercenary comrades, who had been stationed on the battlefield in Bertrandt, escape the pursuit of enemy forces. Clutching a bomb to his body, he'd ultimately carried out a suicide attack on the enemy lines.

And just like that, he'd died in the explosion...or more precisely, he'd pretended to.

Bomb blasts were no big deal as long as you dug a hole to take cover in beforehand.

"'Everyone, keep on living your lives to the fullest, for my sake.' 'Captain, thank you for everything.' 'As my final act, let me repay you for all you've done for me.' My comrades were in tears as I spoke my last words... 'Don't do it, you idiot!' 'Come back!' 'Stop!' they told me... Heh-heh-heh..."

Turns out Rix was kind of a dick.

"But, Captain, everyone—I had to do this. After all, I have a goal that I just can't give up on."

Rix gazed up at the sky with a devilish look on his face.

"That's right...I'm quitting being a mercenary to become a wizard! Why, you may ask? Because being a merc is real rough, and it's all downhill from heeeeeeeeeeeeeeeere!"

The boy cried out from deep in his soul.

"So I don't wanna do this anymore—this life where day after day I don't know if I'm going to live or die! On top of that, mercenaries can't exactly get married, can they?! Who could even imagine a future with someone who might die any day? And that's totally understandable! I wouldn't want that, either, dammit! But when I opened up about these worries to the captain, that bastard just handed me some money, gave me a huge smile and a thumbs-up, and told me, 'Get yourself to a brothel!' No way in hell! I only wanna do that kind of thing with the person I'm going to spend the rest of my life wiiiiiiith!"

Turns out Rix was a bit obsessed, in a creepy way.

"So that's why I'm quitting being a mercenary! Today, I say goodbye to the Black Mercenary Corps and its motto: 'Welcome those who come our way, but chase those who try to leave to the ends of hell'! I'm gonna become a wizard! And luckily, I've got an in!"

As a matter of fact, being a mage was the most marketable profession out there.

Mages proficient in all kinds of magic worked actively in every possible field—politics, economics, research, entertainment, agriculture, manufacturing, infrastructure, and so on.

On top of that, mages had a high standing in society, which came with its own variety of privileges and benefits.

This was in stark contrast to mercenaries, who didn't even know if they'd live to see tomorrow.

"Farewell, Captain... Farewell, everyone in the corps... I'm off to become a wizard. As a mage, I'll have nothing to do with any blood-soaked battlefields. I'll find myself a cute wife and lead a fun and peaceful life. And in the end, I'll die in my nice warm bed, surrounded by my grandchildren. Farewell..."

With that, Rix turned on his heel, making to put the ruins of the battlefield behind him for good. But at that very moment...he sensed someone approaching and quickly hid behind a nearby rock.

When he cautiously peeked out to see who it was...

"Rix! Riiiiiiiiix!"

A dozen or so armed figures, led by a tough-looking, muscular man, were wandering aimlessly around the ruins of the battlefield, searching for something.

"What...? It's Captain Black...and the rest of...the Black Mercenary Corps...?!"

Rix stared wide-eyed at his comrades as he listened in on their conversation.

"Rix! Please! If you're alive out there, please respond! Riiix!"

"Captain, it's no good... You saw what happened, didn't you? In his last moments..."

"After an explosion like that, we probably won't be finding anything but bone fragments... *Sniff...*"

"That Rix... Acting so reckless...for all our sakes...!" The tough, muscular man—Captain Black—broke down into tears on the spot. "Rix! You idiot! Why did you have to die?! You think you have the nerve to go and die before me?! Uwaaaaaaagh!"

There wasn't a soul in the eastern continent who didn't know the name of Captain Black of the Black Mercenary Corps, the strongest mercenary alive.

With his usual hearty demeanor, he was often seen boldly guffawing about something or other with a drink in his hand. No one would imagine such a man collapsing into tears like this.

But now he was bawling in grief over Rix's death.

Seeing Captain Black in this state, Rix couldn't help but feel his heart ache.

"C-Captain..."

Ever since he'd taken in the orphaned Rix three years earlier, Black had truly treated the boy like a son. Rix had learned all sorts of things about being a mercenary from the captain—and from the rest of the corps, too.

To Rix, who didn't have a single blood relative, they were like one big family.

And in one way or another, it was all thanks to the Black Mercenary Corps that Rix had survived up until now.

What the hell am I doing? Can I really just forget everything I owe them and do something so ungrateful?!

Rix took one step toward his comrades, drawn to them like a magnet as they searched for him.

And when he did, memories of the time he'd spent with the Black Mercenary Corps flashed through his mind scene by scene:

"Wait—Captain?! What do you mean, I have to go and hold off that huge enemy battalion all by myself?!"

"You'll be fine, Rix! With your abilities, you'll be able to pull it off! Believe in me, because I believe in you!"

"You've gotta be kidding meeeeee! You just decided where to deploy me by a roll of the dice, didn't you?!"

Memories of the unreasonable requests he'd been constantly undertaking.

"C-Captain?! What the hell were you thinking, using up all the corps' funds in one night?!"

"Heh… Last night, if I hadn't offered it all to my little Arietta, I would have lost everything. But thanks to that, it was the best night of my life…! I don't have a single regret! Gwa-ha-ha!"

"You sex-crazed asshole!"

"You're stiff as always, Rix. But it's fine. We can always earn more money by taking out some enemies."

"Screw you!"

Memories of the absurd situations he'd been constantly subjected to.

"Waaaait! Riiiiix! Don't run awaaaaay!"

"Today, you really gotta come with us to the brothel!"

"It's time to give up your virginity already! Come on, do yourself a favor!"

"Aaaaargh! That's none of your business, you idioooots!"

Memories of the constant foolish quarrels with his comrades.

"Heeeey! Why did you have to go and eat all my food, too?! Just when do you think the next ration supply is?! Do you want me to die?!"

"Brother, bein' a mercenary is all about survival of the fittest! It's your fault for lettin' your guard down!" (smirk)

"I guess I'll just have to eat you, you little brat!"

Memories of his young protégée, who was like a little sister to him, constantly pushing him to the brink of starvation.

"Captain! Captain! How did we end up fighting to the death with this mysterious group of assassins in our own camp?!"

"Heh… No clue! The possibilities are endless!"

"You bastard! Quit messing around!"

"Come on, if you've got time to run your mouth, you've got time to kill one more enemy. Otherwise, you'll be the one to get killed!"

"Aaaaargh! As if I'd die like thiiiiis!"

The constant scenes of carnage.

Nostalgic memories flashed through Rix's mind one after another.

"Yeah…I think I really am done being a mercenary."

That was his conclusion.

It was the only answer, and a simple one.

He'd begun to take a step back toward his comrades but stopped dead in his tracks.

And then Rix again turned on his heel where he stood.

""""RIIIIIIIIIIX!""""""

With his comrades' lamentations at his back, he steeled his expression and left the battlefield behind.

And thus, the young mercenary, Rix, set off for a new world to become a wizard.

No hesitation, no regrets.

Chapter 1
New Encounters

The vast Ford Continent, blessed by the One-Horned Goddess, was divided into four main regions.

The Aldran Empire to the north, controlled by a supreme ruler.

The Kingdom of Forceus, a nation of tradition that governed the southern region.

The East, a conflict zone where various lords, city-states, powerful clans, and tribes lived in turmoil.

And the Principality of Estoria, an island nation on the western edge of the continent.

Estoria was a magical nation with the most highly developed magic arts in the world.

It was also home to the most prestigious magic academy that offered cutting-edge magical research and education: Estoria Academy of Magic.

This was where young people from all reaches of the world who aspired to become mages gathered. It was their holy ground.

And Rix was now on board a ship headed for that very nation…

"To think that just beyond this boundless sea…lies the Principality of Estoria."

Rix, dressed in a simple traveling outfit of a shirt, trousers, and overcoat, stood on the deck of the ship and stared out at the vast sea's horizon as he leaned on the railing.

A pleasant sea breeze was blowing ceaselessly.

The wind caught the ship's sail, which hung from three masts, and the ship cut briskly through the rough waves of the Arlia Sea.

Above Rix was a beautiful clear blue sky.

If he listened closely, he could hear the gentle roar of the sea.

The shifting surface of the water reflected the light of the midday sun and sparkled brilliantly.

The refreshing maritime sight made Rix feel like something was about to begin—something filled with a hope entirely different from before.

"Bleeeeeeeeeegggghhhhhhhh!!"

Rix leaned over the railing and spewed a mess of vomit into the ocean.

"Urgh... I feel sick...! I should have never come here...!"

He was already having some regrets.

While Rix was a battle-hardened mercenary, sea travel had always been a weakness of his.

Owing to this, he immediately became unreliable and useless when it came to marine warfare.

A long journey by ship like this was basically hell on earth for Rix.

"Dammit... I can't do this...!"

At the end of his rope, Rix collapsed to the ground with a *thud*.

"What the hell is this...? This is worse than any battle I've ever experienced...! Am I gonna die? Am I dying...?! In a place like this...?!" he wailed. "Tch... If this is how it's gonna be, then...!"

With a look in his eyes like he had lost all hope in this world, he placed his hand on the hilt of the sword he had hanging at his hip... And then...

"Um... You there... Are you all right?"

"Hey, you... You doing okay?"

*   *   *

Two voices from either side of Rix simultaneously called out to him.

"Hmm?" he said.

"Ah..."

"Oh?"

When he raised his head to look, he saw a girl at his left and a boy standing at his right.

They both appeared to be in their mid-teens, the same as Rix.

The girl was of average height, with flax-colored hair tied in two shoulder-length bundles and kind ultramarine eyes. Her face was beautiful and almost doll-like, yet her lack of makeup and plain looks made her seem a bit unrefined.

But still, her beauty was enough to make Rix's heart skip a beat. More than beautiful, she was cute. Her delicate beauty reminded him of the simplicity of a wildflower blooming in a field.

The boy, meanwhile, had short brown hair and brown eyes and was taller than Rix. He wasn't exactly handsome...but his face was decently good-looking, and he possessed a mysterious charm that drew people to him.

The two were both in traveling garb.

"Who are you two? Muggers? And you're targeting me at my weakest moment...?! Guh?!" cried Rix.

"Obviously not. And anyway, I'm not even with her. But I'm pretty sure that like me, she was just worried about you and wanted to come check if you were okay."

"Y-yes... You look extremely sick..." The girl took a small bottle out from her clothing. Inside it were some kind of pills. "You're seasick, aren't you? If you want, you can use this. You'll feel relief in no time."

"...Oh. Poison, huh? Sure, I'll gladly take you up on that...," said Rix.

"Why would it be poison?! And what do you mean, gladly?!" the boy couldn't help but snap back at Rix's extreme rudeness. "It's for nausea! Magic anti-nausea medicine! It's a pretty famous brand that even I've heard of!"

"Well, she said I'd feel 'relief,' so I just thought..."

"This isn't assisted suicide! Whatever, just hurry up and take it!"

Rix did as the boy urged him to and took the small bottle from the girl.

The medicine worked like a charm. In just a few minutes, Rix was almost completely back to normal.

"Wow, thank you," he told the girl. "You saved my life."

"Saved your life? Ah-ha-ha, no need to exaggerate like that..."

"No, really, I owe you my life! When you found me, I was seconds away from suicide!"

"S-suicide?! How can you say that so casually?!"

"Hmm? I mean, of course I don't actually want to die. But if I had to keep suffering like that, I'd rather...you know. Am I right? I figure anyone else would feel the same..."

"Yeah...I'm kinda starting to regret starting a conversation with you..."

The girl blinked incredulously, and the boy squinted at Rix suspiciously.

"I-in any case, we should introduce ourselves, right? I'm Annie Midir. I'm starting at Estoria Academy of Magic this year. I'm a brand-new first-year student," the girl said with a cheerful smile.

"Oh, okay. I thought so," the boy remarked. "Yeah, most people riding this ship at this time of year must be heading for the academy."

"Which means...you too?"

"Uh-huh. My name's Randy. Randy Ruster. I'm a new student this year at Estoria Academy of Magic, too. Nice to meet you."

The boy, Randy, introduced himself and looked at Rix.

"...Same for you, then?"

"Yeah. I'm Rix Frestat. I've been accepted to Estoria Academy of Magic, which is how I ended up here on my deathbed."

This made Annie and Randy open their eyes wide in astonishment.

"Whaaaat?! You mean you're—?!"

"You're *the* Rix Frestat?!"

In a split second, Rix reflexively reached for the sword at his hip and grew wary out of confusion.

"Wh-why do you know my name?!" he demanded. "Don't tell me the wanted posters for my bounty have made it all the way out here?! Eeeek!"

"No, that's not it! Man, I'm *really* starting to regret talking to you! What's your deal anyway?!"

"U-ummm…calm down, Rix. It's just, you're already pretty famous among the rest of the new students this term," Annie said, trying to soothe Rix. "The academy has what are called scholarship students. Usually, you need to pass an impartial, rigorous entrance exam and aptitude screening to be admitted to Estoria Academy of Magic, but scholarship students are admitted by special invitation and get to ignore that whole process. We don't know how the academy selects these people…but it's said that all scholarship students, without exception, possess *extraordinary magical abilities*."

"Everyone's been talking about how two scholarship students have been admitted this year…," said Randy. "I never would have expected you to be one of them."

"…!"

Rix fell silent with surprise after hearing this.

Indeed, the reason why Rix had decided to quit being a mercenary and become a mage was all because one day, while he'd been happily looting corpses on some battlefield with his comrades, a strange fairy had suddenly appeared before him and handed him a letter.

That letter was now in his pocket, titled "Special Admission Invitation to Estoria Academy of Magic."

He wasn't used to reading anything longer than two sentences, but Rix had fought hard against the urge to fall asleep and had managed to read its contents… He didn't totally get it, but it seemed like he could enter this magic academy for free.

At the time, he'd just figured he had gotten lucky. But after seeing the reaction from these two, he realized it was a pretty big deal.

Rix was, after all, right in the middle of his adolescence.

It felt pretty good to be called "extraordinary," or "special."

In fact, it was something to brag about, wasn't it?

"Oh, really? Extraordinary? I'm *extraordinary*, you say? Stop, you're making me blush!"

"Well…you're not *normal*, in any case."

"Agreed."

Randy narrowed his eyes, and Annie nodded with a vague smile as Rix started to get carried away.

"By the way, what kind of special magic can you use? If you're a scholarship student…you must already be able to use magic, right? Let's hear it."

"S-stop, Randy. Don't you think that's rude to ask? A mage should always keep their cards close to their chest."

Annie admonished Randy, who couldn't help but ask out of curiosity.

"A-about that… The whole magic thing… I can't actually—"

But just as Rix tried to answer that he had never learned to use any magic…

BOOOOOOM!

Even though they were at sea, an earthquake-like impact suddenly shook the ship.

"Whoa!"

"Aaah!"

The force briefly lifted Randy and Annie into the air and sent them tumbling.

"Huh? What was that?" Rix wondered aloud, looking around.

He stood there like nothing had happened.

With his exceptional core strength and stability, it was as if he had been glued to the ship.

"H-huh? Rix…how can you stay so calm…?" Randy asked.

But just then, a shout rang out:

"Monsterrrrr! It's a sea monsterrrrr!"

The next moment, countless columns of water shot up toward the sky from around the ship.

And then from within those columns emerged a giant tentacle, its surface packed with rows of suckers. It was enough to make anyone instinctually reel back in disgust.

Before long, a huge whirlpool was stirred up next to the ship, and out of its center appeared a giant body.

The squid-like creature that dwarfed the ship was the notorious monster that had doomed countless sailors to their watery graves since time immemorial—the Kraken.

Its two gigantic eyes rolled to glare at the people standing on deck.

And then, as if it had just spotted today's feed, the humongous Kraken began getting closer and closer to the ship.

"Wh-whooooaaaaaa?!"

"Ah… Um… Er…"

The passengers were like deer caught in headlights.

Randy fell into a state of panic, while Annie froze in place, dumbfounded.

On the ship's deck with them was a crowd who also seemed to be new students at Estoria Academy of Magic…but they were all simply running around, screaming in terror.

"Dammit, how did this happen?! It's unfathomable that a sea monster would appear in this area of the sea!"

Before long, the captain and what appeared to be the ship's crew came flying onto the deck.

"Wh-what should we do, Captain?!"

"Swords or cannons won't have any effect… Our only hope is to use magic against it!"

"But this area of the sea was supposed to be a safe zone from monsters! We didn't hire a single mage for the crew!"

"Well, find one, dammit—anyone aboard who can use magic! Luckily, this ship is headed for Estoria! There must be someone here who can fight with magic!"

With that, the crew started searching through the passengers for a capable mage.

Rix watched the crew's frantic search and thought, *Mages have all sorts of marketable skills. That naturally means some take on work that relates to combat… But I myself have no plans to do that kind of work in the future!*

That aside, they really needed to do something about that sea monster.

He didn't want to become some giant squid's lunch.

Rix turned back to Randy and Annie, and with a rallying smile, he gave them a thumbs-up. "Okay. It's your turn, guys! Take that thing down with your magic!"

"Y-you're joking, right?!" Randy howled. "Unlike you with your special abilities, we can't use our magic yet! We haven't opened our Spheres!"

"…Spheres?" Rix looked at them blankly.

Annie, shaking in fear, began to explain. "Yes… I'd bet most of the new students on this ship still aren't able to use magic… And even if they could…"

She glanced at the fearsome beast as it neared the ship.

It wasn't clear if she had done so coincidentally or intentionally, but the monster's eyeballs rolled around to meet her gaze.

"Eep…!"

Annie immediately went pale, hugged her body, and started shaking with tears in her eyes.

"Right… I guess you really can't fight that thing, seeing as it's so gross-looking. Tch! If only it had been a *cute* sea monster…!"

"No, that's obviously not the issue at hand here!"

Even in this dire situation, Randy managed to shoot down Rix's ridiculous comment.

Sure enough, all the new students on deck were simply panicking. Not a single one dared to face the monster.

Meanwhile, the monster had now closed in on the ship and was swinging its tentacle high—and bringing it down to slap the deck.

Just then, Annie and Randy saw something they couldn't ignore.

"Ah!"

"That girl…!"

Standing all alone at the edge of the opposite side of the deck was a single girl.

She had distinctive white hair.

Was she stupefied by the sight of the sea monster coming right toward her?

She didn't try to run or hide.

But the sea monster's tentacle was about to come crashing down right above her head…

"Hey! You over there! Watch out!" Randy yelled.

"R-run!" Annie screamed.

But their cries were in vain.

The humongous tentacle was ready to slam down on the girl where she stood…but then:

Slash!

Suddenly, a severed tentacle flew up into the air and was launched off in the other direction.

"Huh?!"

"Wha—?!"

Rix was standing in front of the girl, wielding his unsheathed sword.

He was in position to defend her from the sea monster's attacks.

"R-Rix?!"

"Wh-what?! How did he get over there?!"

Annie and Randy looked surprised as they compared the place where they were standing to where Rix now had appeared.

Now matter how they looked at it, it was a significant distance. There was no way he could have covered it in one move.

But somehow, even though he had just been standing right next to them, he was now all the way over there.

On top of that...judging from what they were seeing, he had also chopped off the sea monster's tentacle with one hit and sent it flying.

"No way... What just happened...?" said Annie.

"Could it be...? Is this his magic?!" cried Randy.

"Teleportation magic, plus powerful sword enchantment magic... both at an extremely high level?!"

"Scholarship students really are something else! That's amazing, Rix!"

As the two of them were getting riled up...

Um... All I did was run up to it and slash it with my sword, like I usually do...

Rix wasn't really sure how he should feel about it.

As a matter of fact, Rix hadn't used even a bit of magic. More like he wasn't able to.

And he had even recently switched out his sword for some random normal sword at a weapons shop. (The sword he was using before had been so dirty and blackened with the blood and grease of the humans and monsters he had fought that he'd been a little embarrassed to use it in front of others.)

All this to say he had simply done what he usually did.

Well, more importantly...

Rix looked behind him. He saw the girl with white hair still standing silently.

There was something odd about her.

Her hair was stark white, the color of burned-out ash. Her skin was as fair as unblemished fresh snowfall. Her narrow eyes were pale blue like ice.

But the girl wasn't looking at anything. Not at Rix who had saved her, nor at the looming sea monster that had just tried to take her life.

The light that filled her eyes was like an infinite void.

She wasn't cowering in fear; she was simply not interested. Not in the sea monster, not even in her own life.

Wh-what's up with this girl...? Rix thought.

The whole thing was so strange that it sent a shiver down Rix's spine.

But even more than that, and despite that—the girl was beautiful. Enough to take your breath away. Her beauty was delicate, almost like that of a fairy. Her silhouette was both trim and voluptuous.

Although she wasn't remotely pretentious, she was constructed almost too perfectly, like a piece of art.

Her blank, unseeing gaze wandered emptily; the sea breeze played with her white hair... It was like something from a postcard. Like a sacred, inviolable piece of magic glasswork, not to be sullied by human hands.

"Are you okay?" Rix asked her.

The battle-hardened mercenary was almost overcome by the urge to keep staring at her forever.

But he returned to combat mode, broke off his gaze from the girl, and turned back to face the sea monster writhing in pain before him.

"It's dangerous, so you should stand back," he warned the girl before focusing on the monster once more.

But then, Rix heard the girl whisper something.

It had barely been clear enough for him to make out.

"...Just stay out of it."

Her whisper was somehow decadently weary, like she had given up on everything in this world.

Huh?

Rix wanted to turn around and ask her what she meant.

BOOM!

But suddenly, the monster before him was enveloped in a raging conflagration that swirled as it burned the creature.

The monster, which had been trying to sink the ship by tangling it in its tentacles, was now flailing violently against the water's surface.

Mysteriously, even when it submerged its burning body in the water, the flames showed no signs of being extinguished.

In its attempt to put out the inextinguishable flames, the monster had begun to rampage and stopped paying attention to the boat.

What is that?! Rix thought, squinting suspiciously as he was buffeted by heat and hot wind.

"Hmph, how unfortunate… You beat me to the first strike."

Before he knew it, a new girl was standing right next to him.

She had long red hair like burning flames and a determined look in her deep crimson eyes.

She had sleek, supple limbs and a tight, lean body, with a kind of raw physical beauty like a ferocious animal stalking its prey.

"And here I thought this would be the perfect opportunity to make my military prowess known to the world in all its splendor," she said.

Huh. This girl seems pretty capable, Rix thought the moment he saw her flawless stance.

It was an undeniably beautiful sight.

There was something wild about her, but not in a savage way. Her beauty, which couldn't hide its nobility, was overflowing with liveliness, vigor, and confidence.

She could be compared to a beautiful pedigreed cat. While the white-haired girl's beauty was like an inorganic art piece, this red-haired girl's beauty was overflowing with vitality.

Judging from the many ornaments attached to her person and the luxurious traveling dress she wore, this girl seemed to belong to some noble family.

And now she was standing next to Rix, lowering her magnificent rapier, which was bathed in sparks.

"I must say, I didn't expect there to be any other brave soul with enough mettle to face the sea monster besides myself… I laud your efforts," she remarked with a smirk. "Heh-heh… And as your reward, I will permit you to introduce yourself to me, boy."

She then gracefully aimed the tip of her rapier at the sea monster.

"Nah, I'll pass," Rix replied simply.

"Th-this is the part where you're supposed to humbly tell me your name, is it not?! You know, I've bestowed quite the honor upon you, boy! Like, it's a big deal! Seriously!"

"Huh? Well, honor doesn't pay the bills… Who are you anyway?"

"Hrmph… To think there are any who do not know my face…and that you would make me stoop to introducing myself first…! Very well, then! It is also the duty of the highborn to display the greatness of their caliber!" the girl announced. "Listen well, and may it be ingrained upon your very soul! My name is Serephina Aldran—the Princess of the Crimson Flame herself!"

The girl, Serephina, introduced herself with a smarmy grin.

"So who?" Rix asked bluntly.

"Whaaat?! You've never heard of me?!" Her eyes welled up with tears of despair. "Ugh…I was under the impression that I am relatively famous… I've never had to introduce myself to someone who didn't know who I was…"

Just then:

"Y-you're *the* Princess Serephina Aldran?!"

"No way! Seriously?!"

From behind them, Annie and Randy broke into hysterics.

Rix and Serephina turned around; apparently, Randy and Annie had come over to bring the white-haired girl away from the line of fire.

They had linked arms with the girl, who still showed no signs of moving.

"Annie? Randy? You know of this Serephina Aldran person?!" Rix asked.

"Yeah, of course! How can you not?!" Randy cried.

"She's the third princess of the Aldran Empire, the strongest military power in the world! She's renowned for her involvement in everything from the military, politics, and foreign affairs at such a young age!"

"I had heard she would be entering Estoria Academy of Magic this year as a new student…!"

Annie and Randy explained, still in awe.

"Oh, *that* Aldran Empire? They don't pay very well, so I've never been a big fan," said Rix. "I mean, where do they get off being so cheap when they're as rich as they are? Maybe people at the top are just stingy by nature. What do you think, Serephina?"

"I think I'd like to cut you down right about now."

With the vein in her temple throbbing angrily, Serephina aimed her rapier at Rix's neck.

Annie and Randy began to panic.

"Oh, forget it," Serephina spat. "I'll allow it! This isn't the time for such bickering!"

Still fuming, she broke her gaze away from Rix and fixed it back on the sea monster. It seemed to have finally put out the flames.

However, only the surface of its body had been burned. The half-baked damage it had suffered only succeeded in enraging it more. And now the monster was glaring at the ship and wriggling its tentacles as if to say there was no way they'd be getting away this time.

At this rate, it was only a matter of time before the ship would be tangled once again in its tentacles and dragged down to the bottom of the sea.

"I decided I'm going to die in bed, surrounded by my grandchildren. I don't want my body to be buried at the bottom of the ocean. We'll just have to take that thing on," said Rix. "Can I count on you to fight with me, Serephina?"

"Hrmph…" Serephina pouted her lips sullenly.

"Wh-what…?"

"Grr… I introduced myself, didn't I? It's simply a universal courtesy to answer an introduction with an introduction, regardless of your social standing. Is it not?"

"Oh, right, sorry! I'm Rix. Rix Frestat."

"Rix, is it? Hmph… A fine name. I'll remember it well."

"Huh?! What's so fine about it?! Pretty sure it's just a plain old name, overused by commoners with no individuality. There must be something wrong with your taste in names."

"I was just trying to pay you a courtesy! Goodness, talking with you is exhausting!" Serephina griped. "In any case, let us take down that thing together! I still have much to accomplish—I shan't be dying here today!"

"Yeah, I feel the same. At the very least, I can't die before I destroy all those dirty magazines I sent in my luggage to the academy dormitory!"

"Don't lump me in with the likes of you! I have half a mind to cut you down for your disrespect!" she howled back at Rix, her face a deep red.

Rix was gazing at Serephina with a serious look like he had found a kindred soul.

"A-anyway… Rix, Princess, if you're going to fight that thing, please be careful!" Randy urged.

"I'm praying for your safe return…!" Annie added.

The two of them retreated, forcibly bringing the still unresponsive white-haired girl along with them.

And so the odd couple of a fighting team was hastily formed, and the battle recommenced.

The Kraken—the scourge of the sea.

Since the dawn of time, with its overwhelming size and beastly strength, the mighty sea monster had struck terror and despair into the hearts of sailors who encountered it before dragging them to their watery graves.

But there was one thing the monster had been unable to predict this time…and that was that both Rix and Serephina were aboard the ship it had set its sights on.

"Hyaaaaaaaaaah!"

With a spirited battle cry, Serephina swung her rapier.

A coil of bright red flames welled forth from the blade, and a huge pillar of fire rose up with overwhelming force and heat.

The swirling flames became a firestorm that assaulted the sea monster, lapping the creature's body as if it had a mind of its own.

"%#%&'%$#!"#$'?><#'$%#~!!"

The Kraken, unable to bear the attack, raised its huge tentacles and swung them down on Serephina.

But Serephina neither panicked nor faltered.

"Not on my watch!"

Once again, she gracefully swung her rapier.

Several fireballs emitted from the blade slammed against the tentacles as they closed in on her, causing massive explosions one after another.

The resulting flames knocked the tentacles back.

Serephina's flame magic was completely overwhelming the sea monster.

"A-amazing… Princess Serephina really has already opened her Sphere…"

"And she isn't even using incantations to cast her magic… She really knows what she's doing!"

Annie and Randy watched Serephina from a distance, their eyes wide.

And they weren't the only ones.

"That person is Serephina Aldran…?"

"Even though she's a new student like us, she's at a totally different level…"

"What strength…! What beauty…!"

"Sh-she's awesome…!"

The other students on the deck were staring at Serephina in admiration.

"…"

That is, except the white-haired girl, who gazed disinterestedly at some other area of the sea.

Nonetheless, Serephina was ecstatic to be basking in the attention of most of the people on the ship.

"Heh-heh. This flame magic is my personal specialty. Go ahead, compliment me more! Sing my praises!"

She puffed up her chest with a proud smirk. However, that confident air was born out of her lack of real experience in battle.

Suddenly, the sea monster shot its tentacles right into Serephina's blind spot.

Tearing through the air with a roar, the powerful attack closed in on Serephina.

"…Hmm?!"

In an instant, Serephina once again enveloped her rapier in flames and aimed to take out the encroaching tentacle.

The rapier and the tentacle clashed fiercely.

But the rapier's blade only cut a few shallow centimeters into the tentacle.

"Grr… It's too thick…! And heavy…!"

Serephina held back the tentacle that had come down on her by blocking it overhead with her rapier.

Serephina, who was already able to use physical enhancement spells, infused magic into her body as she pushed back the tentacle.

But no matter how much she enhanced her strength with magic, the fundamental difference in power between her and the sea monster was too great.

The monster pushed harder, trying to squash Serephina into the ground.

Slash! Slash! Slash!

Suddenly, the tentacle was in four round slices, which flew off in all directions.

"...?!"

"Serephina!"

It was Rix. Swooping in from the side like a gale, he had severed the monster's tentacle with his sword.

Then the Kraken unleashed more tentacles on either side of Rix and started closing in on him.

The monster's speed was almost unfathomable for something so massive—like some kind of illusion.

But Rix's reaction was faster.

"Hup!"

He sliced the tentacle incoming from the left vertically in two, and with a leaping somersault toward the right one, cut it to pieces at the base.

His attack and defense were so swift he barely left behind an afterimage.

Having dealt with the tentacles in a snap, Rix stood next to Serephina to cover her back.

Without leaving a single opening, he readied his sword once again.

"Wow, your flames are amazing! Looks like I can really count on you."

However, Rix's praise hadn't seemed to register with Serephina.

"Serephina?"

She was blinking at Rix in disbelief.

Then, as if she had suddenly realized something, she looked over to the remains of the tentacle Rix had just chopped off.

She took up her rapier, summoned her flames once again, and brought them down upon the remains of the tentacle.

Slash! Her blade cut deeper into the tentacle than her last attempt... but still couldn't cut completely through it.

Having confirmed this, Serephina grinned. "My, my, what a world we live in. There's always someone superior, isn't there?"

"Hmm? Did you say something?" Rix asked.

"Heh... It seems there was some worth in me pushing my way into the academy after all."

"???"

Rix had no idea what Serephina was talking about.

"I suppose that's a scholarship student for you...," said Annie.

"...Rix... Who the hell *are* you...?" Randy muttered.

The two of them were surprised by Rix's power all over again.

"What's with your physical enhancement magic?! It's ridiculously strong...!"

"And that enchantment spell...! Just how much mana did you infuse into your sword...?!"

"H-he's a beast...!"

The other students were similarly flabbergasted, even more so now than after witnessing Serephina's abilities.

Then...

"...Swordsman..."

Something had drawn the white-haired girl's attention. She was looking at Rix.

This girl, who hadn't shown any interest in a single thing—even her own life—was now for some reason staring at him.

"In any case! We can't drag this out, or else the ship won't hold! We need to finish it, and pronto!" said Rix. "Serephina! Bind its movements with your flames!"

"Oh my, now you think you can make me into your little sidekick? What insolence! Well, fine! I'll allow it this time!"

And so Rix and Serephina recommenced the battle.

Serephina stirred up more of her flames and began burning the monster. The flames wriggled like snakes and wrapped around the Kraken's body.

Then Rix, using the immobilized tentacles as his footing, leaped up and brought down a flurry of slashes on the creature.

The sea monster shrieked in agony.

It had realized it was no longer hunting the passengers on the ship—the monster itself had become the hunted. But it was already too late.

"Haaaaaaah!"

Serephina's flames rose up to lash back at a tentacle that tried once again to stop their attacks.

"Yes, this is it!"

Rix's sword swooped down from above and slashed into the monster's weak point—into its eyes and the tender space between them.

The atmosphere trembled with the sound of the monster's death throes.

The Kraken, a symbol of the terror and despair of countless sailors, slowly sank back down to the bottom of the sea...

After everything was over...

"Whoo-hooooooo! Rix, you saved our lives back there!"

"Thank you, Rix! Thank you so much!"

"Whoa?!"

Annie and Randy, with tears in their eyes, ran up and hugged the flustered Rix from both sides.

The students, the captain, and the sailors were also crying in relief as they embraced each other.

Hmm? What about that girl...?

Rix suddenly remembered the white-haired girl, whose name he still didn't know. He struggled to look around for her while Randy and Annie jostled him.

Then...

"..."

...he caught sight of the white-haired girl silently descending the stairs that headed belowdecks.

It was as if she had absolutely no interest in any of the merrymaking and hustle and bustle on deck.

Or—she was trying to escape it.

It wasn't like Rix expected her to thank him or be happy about the situation. Not like he expected some new event to get triggered with her or anything.

Okay, sorry. That's a lie. I did expect some of that. I am a guy, after all.

Anyway, that aside...

Actually, just forget it.

"...She really is a strange one," Rix said to himself as he watched the girl walk away.

———

"Excellent work, Princess. Truly, a magnificent display," said a woman in a maid outfit who appeared to be one of Serephina's retainers.

Serephina pouted. "Hrmph. Enough with the flattery. No matter how you look at it, I was merely the backup."

"Ah-ha-ha, I suppose so," the retainer replied.

"Isn't this the part where you're supposed to refute what I said and tell me I was amazing?!"

Tears of despair sprang to Serephina's eyes.

But soon enough, she was back to a serious expression as she whispered secretively to her retainer, "Still, there were some fruits to my labor... You catch my drift, don't you?"

"Yes. Please give us some time. We will thoroughly investigate the boy...this scholarship student, Rix Frestat."

"Please do." Serephina nodded triumphantly. "I see now how he could have been chosen for a scholarship over me. If I am going to take control of the Aldran Empire and bring the rest of the world into my grasp...I'll need a man like him in my army. His power will surely be a boon to my military pursuits. While we are at the academy, I'll make him mine, by any means necessary. I'll find a way, no matter what. Heh-heh-heh."

"Oh? It's rare for you to make such statements, Princess," the retainer remarked. "You seem quite charmed by this boy... He must have caught your attention, yes?"

"What?! I-it's not as if I like him or anything! That's not it at all!" Serephina countered. "This has nothing to do with how my heart skipped a beat because that was the first time I'd ever been protected by someone! I—I think of him as a subordinate! An underling! A pawn!"

"If you say so, Princess."

Serephina, red in the face, waved her arms frantically, but her retainer simply shot her an exasperated stare.

Meanwhile, in a part of the sea far away from Rix's boat...a hooded figure wearing a black robe stood suspended on the water's surface—directly on the water, not supported by anything.

"...That didn't turn out as expected," the mysterious figure whispered scornfully.

The figure turned on their heel and began walking.

Their image wavered like a mirage.

"Well, no matter. I do have a bad habit of getting ahead of myself," they said to no one in particular. "There's no need to rush. If *that's* the case, there are many ways to deal with it. And I have plenty of time... as long as they're at that academy."

Then the figure disappeared completely.

———————

Wanting to leave the battlefield behind and live a peaceful life, Rix had decided to become a mage.

However, he had yet to realize the dark clouds that were already beginning to gather over his grand scheme.

Chapter 2
Estoria Academy of Magic

The Isle of Lodis—an island that was itself considered its own small-scale continent, governed by the Principality of Estoria.

Rix's ship sailed from the Levar Peninsula, which lay on the eastern edge of the Isle of Lodis, south through the Bay of Orth on the continental side of the island, and arrived at a large city port.

It landed at the city of Estorheim: the capital of the Principality of Estoria.

The atmosphere was different from that of the Aldran Empire, which was respected for its quality construction and unadorned austerity, and still different from the Kingdom of Forceus, which boasted beautiful old-fashioned architecture reminiscent of its traditional aristocracy.

The city was on the cutting edge of the age.

The city streets were organized in a grid pattern, with houses and buildings with many spires, arches, and sharp-angled roofs lining the roads. The architecture was luxurious and artistic yet sophisticated.

The city of Estorheim was generally divided into four main districts.

First, in the south was the industrial district. It was a part of the city that never slept, and it housed the ports of entry—which connected the principality to the rest of the continent—Adventurers Guilds, and business districts, all of which operated at all hours of the day.

Next, in the east was the residential district. There were many public squares and natural parks, and compared to the southern district, it had a calm and relaxed atmosphere.

To the north was the governmental district. All of Estoria's administrative facilities were housed here, including Estorland Palace where the ruler of Estoria resided, the aristocracy's townhouses, consulates of various kingdoms, and other administrative agencies. The area's architecture and atmosphere were refined and gorgeous.

Then, away from the hustle and bustle of the rest of the city was Estoria Academy of Magic, in the western suburbs.

The academy was a three-year boarding school for prospective mages and the world's leading magical research institution.

And as fate would have it, Rix was heading for that very academy, together with Annie and Randy.

Using a stagecoach that regularly traveled back and forth from the nearby student district, they meandered through the school route, enveloped by deep, silent forests, before finally reaching the front gate of the academy.

"So this is Estoria Academy of Magic," said Rix.

Among the lush, beautiful natural landscape, Rix and the others were greeted by a huge school building that resembled a castle, standing tall in the vast grounds of the academy, which were surrounded by a large wall.

———

After passing through the tall, ornate gate, Rix and his classmates were met in the front yard by older students who were to act as their guides, and they were soon being led through the school building.

The school building was built primarily of stone, and its interior was luxurious like some kind of aristocratic mansion.

Eventually, they made their way to the school office. There, Rix, Randy, and Annie parted ways temporarily to individually go over the various procedures relating to their matriculation and entrance into the dormitories.

Once that was completed, Rix was provided with a white robe and instructed to put it on and head to a large hall.

Following a map of the school grounds, he walked through the labyrinthian building before finally reaching the hall.

It looked like the place where the school held banquets and other large gatherings. The space was extravagant and spacious, with high ceilings.

There were already many people who looked like new students, like Rix, gathered in the hall.

There must have been about one hundred and twenty people in attendance.

Some were wearing the same white robe as Rix, while others were in blue or red robes. Among the three colors, there were forty students each, all chatting pleasantly.

"Heeey! Rix! Over here!"

"Riiix!"

Rix turned around toward the voices calling his name. Randy and Annie were there, waving over at him. They were both wearing the same white robe as Rix.

"Ha! So you're in the White Class, too!"

"Hee-hee! Looks like we'll be spending the next three years together!"

Randy and Annie looked happily at Rix, but he just stared back at them blankly.

"What, you didn't know? The academy is divided into three classes: White, Red, and Blue. Then each color has all their lessons together," said Randy. "The dormitories are separated by each color, too."

"Ah-ha-ha, the dorms are also separated by gender, of course," added Annie. "But still, students who end up in the same class inevitably spend a lot more time together."

"I see… So the robe colors are how we're separated into the class and dormitory we belong to." Rix frowned. "But white, huh…? White Class…? Hrm…"

"What's wrong? Something bothering you? What, you don't want to be in the same class as us?" Randy asked.

"No, I'm happy about that part. I was just thinking that if I could choose, I'd rather be in the Red Class."

"Huh? Why's that?"

"I mean, blood spatter kinda stands out against white robes, right?"

"…"

"…"

"And like, if you're wearing red, it's a little less, y'know?" Rix added cheerfully, even though Randy and Annie were recoiling.

"A-a little less *what*…?" Annie stammered.

"Does every single thing you say have to be so disturbing and violent?" Randy asked.

Then:

"Oh-ho-ho! It has been too long! Waiting for me, were you?"

A bright and rather pompous-sounding voice called out to them.

They didn't even need to turn around to know it was Serephina.

She wore a white robe, the same as Rix and the others, and stood in a commanding and fearless pose with her arms crossed.

"P-Princess?!"

"Princess Serephina?! U-um, how is Her Highness doing on this fine day?"

Annie and Randy hurriedly straightened their postures to greet her.

"Hmph… No need for titles or all that politeness," Serephina told them. "Here, I am not royalty—I'm simply Serephina. I'm just another student striving to master the magic arts, the same as you."

"True. We're all students here, yeah? So no need to get all worked up or anxious around each other!" Rix cheekily wrapped his arm around Serephina's shoulder, giving a bright smile and a thumbs-up. "Isn't that right, Serephina?"

"Perhaps you should mind your manners a bit more... On second thought, fine. I'll allow this." Serephina's face stiffened as she stared back at Rix.

"Um...so it looks like you're in the White Class with us, too, Serephina...," Annie noted.

"Correct. To be honest, I believe the noble colors of the Red Class would suit me much better... But it seems I was fated to wear white instead," Serephina said with an exaggerated nod. "Thanks to that, it looks like I'll be spending the next three years with you all. I am most pleased."

"Man...who would have thought four people who randomly met on that ship would somehow end up in the same class...? It almost feels like someone set this up, am I right?" Randy joked.

Serephina's shoulders twitched, then she started to flail her arms and rattle off an explanation.

"C-certainly not!! There's absolutely no way that, for instance, I was originally in the Red Class but used my wealth and influence to be moved into the same class as Rix! That is simply impossible! What a preposterous idea!"

"Pfft! She's right! What are you even suggesting, Randy?" said Rix. "There's no way all that overly specific stuff that Serephina just said is what actually happened! Get real! Ah-ha-ha-ha-ha!"

And in response...

"...This is giving me a headache."

"Ah-ha-ha-ha... It seems like the next three years are going to be pretty interesting..."

…Randy glared and sighed back at them, while Annie gave them a vague smile.

Then…

"Hey… You think you can ignore me, you twit?!"

Suddenly, someone was yelling a short distance away. The crowd of students began murmuring to one another.

Rix and the others turned around to see a few students standing alone in the center of a ring of other students who had moved away in order to not get involved.

One of them was the white-haired girl who had been on the ship. She was wearing a white robe that matched her hair. It looked like she had become part of the White Class, too.

Threatening her was a male student in a red robe, who was grabbing her by her lapels and holding her up.

He was bigger and taller than Randy, with a toned physique that indicated clearly that he'd had some martial arts training. He had haughty features, and the grin on his face made it seem like he was looking down on everyone. He was glaring at the white-haired girl with contempt.

"You listenin' now? Maybe you didn't hear me the first time, so I'll tell you again," he said. "I, Gordon Grolyle, have taken a liking to a lowly common girl like you. It's an honor you don't even deserve."

"…"

"That means from today, I've decided you belong to me," he continued. "You'll move from the White Class to the Red Class. And you'll stay in my room with me. I'll make sure to take good care of you every night. You may think I'm crazy, but it'll be easy enough using my family's power. What, aren't you happy? You've won the favor of a Grolyle, after all. I'll keep you as a pet, at least until I get sick of you. Heh-heh-heh…"

Two male students in the same red robes as Gordon who appeared to be his toadies grinned creepily.

"Gya-ha-ha! Hey, Gordon, don't break her in too hard before you share her with us!" one said.

"Yeah, yeah! She's a real stunner, after all!" another chimed in.

"Man, did you get a good look at her face? Oof, I don't think I've ever seen one as pretty as her!"

One of the boys sidled up to her, took her chin in his hand, and jerked it up.

"No kidding! Compared to this one, all the other girls here look like potatoes!"

The other boy started rubbing his hands over the girl's hips and legs.

It was unbelievably insulting, unbelievably humiliating.

And yet...

"..."

...the girl was silent. Unresponsive. It was like she couldn't even see the male students surrounding her.

She didn't scream for them to stop, and she didn't look frightened, either. She wasn't trying to act brave or defy her tormentors. She didn't obey them to avoid getting hurt or try to flatter them.

She didn't give Gordon and his friends a single reaction they were hoping to see. So it was no surprise that he was starting to get a little angry.

"Hey...come on, aren't you gonna say anything? Huh?!"

And then...the white-haired girl, who had looked like she was frozen in time up until that moment, suddenly spoke:

"...Whatever."

"Huh?" said Gordon.

"Who cares?" the girl said. "Do whatever you want."

"?!"

She didn't even glance at Gordon or his friends. She was hopelessly disinterested to her core—in them and in herself.

Her attitude was enough to really rub Gordon's pride the wrong way.

"Don't get cocky with me. You're just a common Fool who hasn't even opened her Sphere yet!"

As he grabbed the girl by the lapels, the look in his eye was getting more and more dangerous.

"I guess there are scum like that everywhere you go," Serephina spat disgustedly. "I can't bear to watch. They're not even worth calling the teachers over. I'll deal with them myself."

"Wait." Rix grabbed Serephina by the shoulder.

"Don't try and stop me, Rix."

"Listen, just calm down. From what I can tell, you're not the most socially adept. No matter what we do, this is probably going to turn into a fight."

Rix pointed at Serephina's hand, which was resting on the hilt of her rapier.

"Leave this one to me, all right? Don't worry; I'm used to dealing with situations like this." Rix winked confidently.

"Hrmph… If you insist…"

Then Randy came up to Rix and gave him a warning.

"Rix, watch out. That guy said he's a Grolyle."

"Yeah? So what?"

"I'll spare you the details, but they're a noble and pretty powerful family in the magical community. If you don't handle this carefully, it could mess up your life here at the academy going forward."

"It's fine, don't worry! I'll settle this peacefully. Just sit back and watch, okay?"

Rix left Randy and Annie behind with worried looks on their faces and casually walked up to Gordon.

"Hmph, maybe a cocky brat like you needs to be taught a lesson to get it through your head!" Gordon sneered.

Just as Gordon was raising his fist above his head at the girl who wasn't resisting him whatsoever…

"Stop! Stoppp! You over there! Violence isn't the answer!"

…Rix waltzed right up between the two of them.

"Huh?! Who the hell are you?!"

Gordon's face looked even scarier once the interloper barged in.

Rix smiled gently and spoke sincerely. "Humans have this wonderful thing called language. As long as we use our words, I think we can find a good solution together. What I'm saying is—"

Gordon wasn't hearing a word of it. Suddenly, he posed like he was getting ready to punch Rix and shut him up.

"—screw youuuuuuuuu!"

However, Rix was faster. He plunged his fist into Gordon's face with everything he had.

"Buuuuuuuuuuh?!"

Gordon was blown away, tumbling head over heels.

The crowd of students surrounding them quickly parted to avoid Gordon as he flew toward them.

Eventually, he slammed against the wall and fell to the floor.

"G-Gordon?!"

"You bastard! How dare you—"

Gordon's lackeys flew at Rix.

"Stop it, you guys!" Rix knocked down the one coming at him from the right. "Violence won't solve anything!"

He then kicked the one coming at him from the left. "If we stay calm and talk it out, we'll definitely find some way to understand each other!"

"That's not convincing at aaaaaaallllllll!"

Randy felt practically obligated to comment as Rix pleaded earnestly with Gordon and the others, who lay slumped and lifeless around him.

"Hey! Rix! Didn't you say you were going to settle this peacefully?!"

"Huh?" Rix looked taken aback and pointed at the blade hanging from his hip. "I didn't draw my sword, did I?"

"*That's* your standard for 'peaceful'?!" Randy was tearing at his own hair in frustration.

"Even I wasn't going to go that far," said Serephina, staring exasperatedly.

"Oh no, oh no…" Annie was clearly flustered.

After a moment…

"B-bastard…! You think you can mess with me…?!"

Having seemingly taken less damage than everyone had expected, Gordon was staggering to his feet.

His face was bright red and demonic. Now he had completely lost it.

Having already regained stable footing, he went up to Rix and glared down at him.

"I'll kill you! I swear, I'll kill you!"

"Hmm? Hang on, have you killed a person before? That makes two of us!"

Rix blinked in surprise, while Gordon seemed momentarily at a loss for words.

"Huh? Wh-what…are you talkin' about…?" he stammered.

"It seems like we could be good friends after all! Nice!" Rix extended his hand for a handshake.

Though he was saying something outrageous, Rix's expression remained calm.

To Gordon, that look on Rix's face was somehow very…

"I'll kill yooooouuuuu!!"

To stifle that feeling that had almost crept into his mind, Gordon flew into a rage and started to cast a spell.

He summoned a fierce ball of lightning in his right hand, and just as he prepared to bring it down on Rix…

"That's enough!"

Thud!

Suddenly, a tremendous weight of gravity was applied to Rix's and Gordon's shoulders.

Their bodies became heavy. Too heavy. This enormous weight felt like their flesh and bone had turned into lead. They could no longer stand.

"Oof?!"

Unable to bear the weight, Gordon collapsed on the spot.

"…Guh?! What is this…?!"

Rix fell to one knee.

"Oh?"

All of the sudden, they noticed a man standing on the stage at the far end of the large hall.

He was eyeing Rix, who had been able to withstand the increased gravity, with great interest.

This handsome man was dressed in a black robe. He had a tall, large, and stocky build. His bronze-red hair looked like a lion's mane, and his golden eyes shone with intellect. His appearance was immaculate. The aura he gave off made it clear he was no ordinary man, even to the untrained eye.

Seeing that the situation had settled, the man snapped his fingers.

With that signal, the gravity that had been holding down Rix and Gordon suddenly disappeared.

Then the man began to address the buzzing hall full of new students.

"I am the headmaster of Estoria Academy of Magic: Grand Master Jake Dryson!"

A murmur spread throughout the hall.

Headmaster Jake began making an announcement.

"You are young! It is only natural that you have that youthful enthusiasm! In fact, it is best to experience it fully while you are still young! For that in itself is the essence of youth!" he boomed. "However, there are many things that cannot be written off as mere youthful enthusiasm! Among them is personal fights between students, using magic! Magical combat on school grounds without permission is prohibited according to the school rules and regulations! If you break this rule, you may be severely punished. And that may, under certain circumstances, lead to expulsion from the academy! However, this is your first day, so I will make a special exception! In fact, it's rather cute to see the boys getting all hotheaded and beating each other up! Yes, I'm glad to see you so full of vim and vigor!

"But let us move on! Everyone, please return to your designated spots! We are about to start the entrance ceremony! Welcome to Estoria Academy of Magic! Your glorious journey begins here!"

Headmaster Jake was the kind of man who was constantly giving off an air of passion with his entire body that felt almost excessive.

But one could instinctually tell that neither Rix nor Serephina, nor Gordon, nor even all the students put together, would be any match for him.

They could feel that Headmaster Jake was an enormously powerful mage, down to their very souls.

"Tch..."

Having understood this, Gordon clicked his tongue and returned to his spot with the Red Class.

As he passed by Rix, he spat a final threat at him.

"You may have been lucky this time, but I'm still gonna kill you. And don't you forget it."

"Heh... You expect me to remember that when I can't even remember my multiplication tables?"

"I said don't forget it!"

Gordon squared his shoulders as he walked away.

Thus, the situation was somehow resolved for the time being.

The entrance ceremony was nothing special.

It simply went through the standard type of ceremonial procedure that was common everywhere, part by part, in the usual order.

At the end of the ceremony, Headmaster Jake gave a closing speech.

"And so! I want you to all be conscious of the meaning and responsibility that lies with learning magic! With power comes responsibility! And those with great abilities have an obligation to use those abilities to give back to the world! And so you must not use those powers, or those abilities, in your own self-interest! Having been accepted into this academy, you already possess great power! You are brimming with a talent unknown to so many others! So while you are here at this academy, you must think hard on how you will devote yourself going forward, how you will use that power, and what type of life you want to live! As you already are aware, in recent years, a deplorable group of alumni that calls itself the Faith Faction has been building its power from within this very academy! Yes, that very same group, its members no longer worthy of being called mages, worships the evil Dusk Demon as their founder and irresponsibly seeks to use forbidden magic in pursuit of easy power!

"I implore you to hold fast to your beliefs and not give in to such temptations…"

To Rix, Headmaster Jake's speech, given with a magically amplified voice, was just like a lullaby. It was making him sleepy.

Rix had gotten used to sleeping standing up from his mercenary days. Unable to resist his drowsiness, he was about to lose consciousness completely when—

"You… What is your goal?"

—a sudden voice from beside him woke him back up.

When he looked next to him…he saw the white-haired girl standing there.

Rix blinked in disbelief; he hadn't expected her to talk to him. The girl didn't bother to look his way.

"That time on the boat, you saved me and indebted me to you. And earlier, you did the same thing once again. So what is your goal? What is it you want? My body?" she asked. "Fine. If you're okay with a plain body like this, then go ahead."

"Heh… I'm not that kind of guy. I'll only do that kind of thing with someone I've committed my future to!"

"…Hmph. Gross."

"Guh?!"

The girl's emotionless words pierced straight into Rix's heart.

"If not my body, then what do you want? A feeling of righteousness, having saved the weak? A sense of superiority, having defeated the strong? To fulfill your vanity or self-esteem by standing out? Either way, how boring."

"Um… Does it have to be so complicated?" Rix scratched his head at the girl's twisted way of wording things. "Fortunately for me, I have some measure of power. And I saw someone I could help within the limits of that power. In that situation, is it so strange to go ahead and save that person?"

"…"

The girl stayed silent.

After wondering whether he should go on, Rix decided to say what was on his mind.

"I dunno… I sorta felt like you were saying, 'Somebody help me.'"

At that moment, the girl's expression wavered almost imperceptibly.

However, she immediately returned to her stone-faced expression and mumbled, "…What made you think that?"

"Just a feeling" was Rix's vague answer. "And I'm usually right. Thanks to that, I've survived this long."

The girl stayed silent for a while.

On the stage, Headmaster Jake was still giving his closing speech.

Finally, the white-haired girl responded.

"Disgusting..."

Her whisper cut sharp as a knife as it left her dainty lips. Sharper than a sword made of the finest mithril.

"You're really gross, you know that? You disgust me. Never speak to me again," she spat.

"Please stop... This is more painful than any wound I ever got on the battlefield..."

Rix began trembling as his eyes welled with tears.

Man... This girl is unapproachable from all angles, isn't she?

Calling her beautiful would be an understatement. And Rix couldn't deny that he wanted to get to know her better.

Regardless, they would still be spending the next three years together in the White Class.

He wanted to have a good relationship with his fellow classmates... That was his true, unabashed desire.

Maybe getting along with her is a hopeless endeavor... I'll just have to find some way to keep my distance from her..., Rix thought with a sigh.

Then out of nowhere, the girl whispered something strange: "Shino. Shino Whytenight."

"Hmm?"

"...That's my name. You don't need to bother remembering it. But I need to introduce myself to someone if I'm going to thank them, don't I?" The girl—Shino—emotionlessly went on in spite of Rix's visible bewilderment. "I'll say it once for good measure—thank you. But I'll leave it at that."

She said it almost as if talking to herself, not even bothering to look Rix's way.

With that, Shino shut her mouth. She went back to staring blankly into space, as if she had completely lost interest in Rix.

"..."

For a moment, Rix idly scratched his head while he stared at Shino's profile.

After a while, he thought, *She's a strange one...*

He was sure that if Randy, Annie, or Serephina had heard that, they'd all say "You're one to talk!"

"And so, burn brightly, young minds!" the headmaster boomed. "Celebrate your youth with everything you have and live without regrets!"

Finally, Headmaster Jake's long speech came to an end.

Chapter 3
Unlocking the Sphere

The next day, the students left the school building and cut across the beautiful garden past a statue of the One-Horned Goddess to attend a special lecture—one the academy designated as their first class.

"That girl was Shino Whytenight?! Seriously?!"

Randy's hysterical yell rang out across the grounds.
"Do you know her, Randy?" Rix asked, walking alongside his friend.
Randy nodded. "Yeah, I know of her. She's the same as you."
"The same as me?"
"She's a scholarship student. So that means she also has some kind of special magical ability."
Annie and Serephina were behind Rix when Serephina chimed in.
"But isn't it strange? If she's a scholarship student, shouldn't she have been able to deal with that sea monster and with that idiot Gordon somehow on her own...?"
"M-maybe she was scared? She is just one girl, after all...," Annie said, peering forward.
About a dozen meters in front of them, they spotted the white-haired girl, Shino, walking with her back to them.

"Hrm, she wasn't exactly cowering in fear, from what I could tell," Rix mused.

"Then what is it? Why didn't she resist?" Randy asked.

"Maybe she simply can't use magic yet? I mean, I can't yet, either."

"Ha-ha-ha! C'mon, Rix! Good one."

"Oh, stop! Really, you and your jokes! Oh-ho-ho!"

Randy and Serephina didn't take Rix's statement seriously at all.

"But man, the White Class's level is really high this year!" said Randy. "We've got you, Serephina, and another scholarship student in Shino, too! I'm not sure I'm gonna be able to keep up with you guys…"

"Ah-ha-ha, I feel the same, Randy… I'm going to have to try my best to keep up even a little with Rix and Serephina…"

"Oh-ho! Best make sure to diligently apply yourself! And if there's anything you want me to teach you, just say the word. I would be glad to help you out personally as a fellow student. Consider it an honor!"

"By the way, why are you guys lumping me in with the high achievers? Like I said, I can't even…"

As the group chitchatted, they caught sight of their destination, a magic ceremonial ground called the Stone Circle.

Estoria Academy of Magic was a three-year boarding school.

Over those three years, students gained class credits required for graduation and, after passing a certification exam, could become a Rank Four Estoria Certified Mage. In other words, they earned the certification that proved they were competent and became able to enter the workforce.

At the academy, students took classes on nine basic subjects:

Physical enhancement magic
Black magic
White magic
Summoning magic
Magic potions
Magic tool craftsmanship

Magical combat

History of magic

Ancient languages

Ultimately, mages would move on to specialize in their own subject of choice and develop their own personal magic, but these nine subjects acted as the basic foundation of all magic, and therefore the students had to master them.

However, before even beginning to learn these subjects, there was one prerequisite class—the Sphere Unlocking Rite.

And it was the most important rite for turning from an ordinary human into a mage.

"Okay, everyone! I hope you've all come mentally prepared!"

Standing in front of the students of the White Class who had gathered at the Stone Circle was the young female professor in charge of the Sphere Unlocking Rite—Professor Anna Piyonelle. She was smiling cheerfully and waving her hand.

The robe Professor Anna was wearing was black and different from the ones the students wore.

It was proof that she was a full-fledged, certified mage.

"Apparently, Professor Anna is usually in charge of the summoning magic class. But since she's an all-rounder with deep knowledge about all kinds of magic, they also put her in charge of our Sphere Unlocking Rite."

"Oh yeah?"

Rix was only half listening to Randy's explanation when Anna began speaking.

"Today, we will be opening the new students' Spheres!" she announced. "That's the one thing we will be working on in today's class, so please be sure to concentrate! It may be a little boring for anyone who has already opened their Sphere, but later I'd like to use you all as examples to show what an actual opened Sphere looks like. Steel your nerves!"

"Oh-ho, Rix, are your nerves steeled?" whispered Serephina.

"No need."

"I see... I should have expected as much. You have no need for special preparation, I take it?"

"Uh, no, I'm just saying..."

There still seemed to be some kind of misunderstanding between them, which baffled Rix all over again.

Meanwhile, Professor Anna continued. "Anyway, those who have passed the academy's entrance examination should know this already, but...allow me to review with a quiz. What exactly is the Sphere? Yes, over there... Annie."

"Oh! Yes, ma'am!" Annie hurried to stand up and answer. "The Sphere...refers to a supersensory phenomenon and its surrounding area that goes beyond the normal five human senses and the sixth sense at the level of premonition and intuition. It is what we would call a seventh or eighth sense. More concretely, among the three elements that make up life—the material, the astral, and the aetherial—it is an astral and aetherial body removed from the material realm...in other words, a supersensory perception possessed by the human soul."

"Yes, well done." Professor Anna clapped her hands. "Annie is correct. What we call the Sphere is the soul's supersensory perception that goes beyond the material realm. Since the Sphere is free from the yoke of the physical world, it isn't restricted by any of the laws of physics. That is to say, mages are *omnipotent* within the boundaries of their own Sphere. Within the Sphere, one can command and control every phenomenon. And that very command and control of phenomena within the Sphere is what we call magic. How does one expand their Sphere? And how does one strengthen its power? These are some of the eternal questions a mage will face over the span of their lifetime."

Oh, okay... I have no idea what she's talking about, thought Rix.

He gave up on trying to understand. In fact, he was feeling pretty sleepy.

"Though it may be taken for granted, every human possesses a Sphere," the professor added. "After all, there is no such thing as a human without a soul. However...unfortunately, only an extremely small number of those with a Sphere have one that will allow them to be competent as a mage. This is because it is too difficult to use magic with a poor-quality Sphere."

The students who still hadn't opened their Spheres went pale.

"But please don't worry," she went on. "You new students are all here today because you have passed the academy's strict aptitude test. Your very presence means you already possess a Sphere of the minimum qualities required to become a mage. Beyond that, all else depends on how much effort you put in."

That appeared to reassure the new students.

Randy let out a sigh of relief. "Whew... Looks like I won't need to do the walk of shame back to my hometown after all."

"Ordinarily, humans are not only unable to control this Sphere that is indispensable to using magic, but they also can neither see nor feel it. Do you know the reason why? How about you, Randy?" asked Professor Anna.

"Huh?! Me?! Um...?!" Having suddenly been called on, Randy hurried to rack his brain for an answer. "U-um, it's because...this is the material world, and...since humans physically exist in that world...the other five senses get in the way, so they don't notice they have the Sphere because it exists beyond the physical realm... or something like that?"

"Yes, that's correct! Well done." Professor Anna clapped once again. "That's right. Ordinary humans are unable to notice the existence of their Spheres. And that's why ordinary humans are unable to use magic," she explained. "Accordingly, the first step toward becoming a mage is to awaken to the existence of the supersensory perception that is the Sphere. And this is called opening the Sphere. Now, regarding how to open this ever-so-crucial Sphere..."

"Hmph. You use that stuff, right? That pitiful excuse for a potion," came a sarcastic voice from among the White Class.

Everyone turned their attention to the speaker...a high-strung-looking boy with swept-back blond hair and glasses.

"Fool's Elixir," he scoffed. "You'd think people would be embarrassed to rely on some potion in order to become a mage."

"You're...Alfred, correct? Of the Lordston family?"

"I'm not surprised you've heard of us. We are famous...and our power is incomparable to these dime-a-dozen wannabe mages. I'll have you know I've already opened my Sphere. All on my own, of course," he said snidely while pushing his glasses up.

The students started to murmur.

"That jerk...! He thinks he's so much better than us...!" Randy growled in irritation, balling his fists in anger.

"..." Annie was looking down forlornly.

"Hmph...what a narrow-minded little boy. I, too, have opened my Sphere, and I'm proud of it. So who cares about whether others use the Fool's Elixir?" Serephina added, although her response was somewhat contradictory.

Uh...which part am I supposed to be mad about, again?! wondered Rix, the only one who was still totally lost.

The mood had shifted against Alfred in one form or another.

"In fact, there is some truth to Alfred's statement." Professor Anna began to try to settle the group. "Originally, the Sphere was something that was only finally awakened after long years of strict spiritual training. From the point of view of those who opened their Spheres in that way, it may feel unfair to be able to unlock the Sphere with the Fool's Elixir. However, opening the Sphere on one's own requires a person to train continuously from a very young age. And the older someone gets, the more they are bound by their view of their world and the limitations of their own body, and thus it becomes more and more difficult to break down those prejudices. Furthermore…typically only rich noble families are able to train their children in magic from such a young age. That is why magic has been a privilege of the noble class for so long."

"…"

"But thanks to a certain mage's development of the Fool's Elixir, that has all changed," she added. "Now even commoners can become mages…and as a result, there are many more mages than ever before. In turn, we've been able to achieve unprecedented progress and development in magic. We mages are the ones who unravel the truths of this world. I believe that is precisely why the Fool's Elixir has its own legitimate significance. So for now, could you please set aside your misgivings?"

Professor Anna wore a gentle smile.

Unable to come up with a valid counterargument, Alfred turned away.

"H-hmph! It's all because of that Fool's Elixir that we've got more clueless idiots like the Faith Faction becoming mages!" he scoffed. "Well, do what you want. Not like it matters if I disagree with the academy's curriculum anyway!"

"Heh-heh, thank you for your understanding. Let's go ahead and get started."

Now that this slight disturbance had been dealt with…it was time to move on to the ritual that would allow the students to open their Spheres.

First, Professor Anna handed each student a small bottle filled with a strangely colored liquid potion.

Everyone gazed at theirs curiously.

"Did you all get one? That in your hand is the Fool's Elixir, which will help you to open your Sphere," Professor Anna explained. "Even if you have already opened your Sphere, please use the potion and try facing your Sphere from a new perspective. If you do, I'm certain you will discover something new and grow."

Rix and Serephina also held the Fool's Elixir in their hands.

Even Alfred, who had been so negative about it, had reluctantly received one.

"Allow me to remind you that simply drinking the potion is not enough to awaken the Sphere—it's not a miracle drink, after all," the professor told her students. "Actually, the potion is more akin to poison. If you use it incorrectly, you could die."

""""?!?!?!""""""

Hearing her say something so terrifying with a smile, the already restless students went pale again.

"It is a type of anesthetic, formulated with a combination of various magical ingredients, including mandrake oil, forget-me-not, *Psilocybe venenata*, Hydra venom, and so on. After taking a dose, the five senses of your physical body will become numb. That means the senses outside the physical—namely, those that sense your Sphere— will become easier to use. Please do your best to grasp it. Notice it. Awaken to this new sensation residing within yourselves that you have never been conscious of before. For that is the first step in your journey toward becoming a mage."

Professor Anna gazed warmly at her charges.

"As the potion is very strong, first take only one drop onto your finger and lick it. If after that, you still haven't grasped the sensation of your Sphere, you may take one more drop. Since you all possess a considerable inclination toward the magic arts, I believe all should be able to grasp their Spheres with this dose…but if you still haven't after two drops, please tell me."

With this, the new students took the first step on their journey to become mages—the ritual to open their Spheres began.

The class used the potion according to Professor Anna's directions.

Then, seated in a large circle—the boys cross-legged, the girls on their heels—the students closed their eyes.

As instructed, they repeated a special breathing rhythm to calm the mind.

Then the potions began to take effect one after another.

"P-Professor...I'm scared...! I feel like I'm going to disappear...!"

"I-I'm falling... My body is falling away...!"

"Eek... A-aah...!"

Shouts of confusion rang out as everyone's five senses started to turn numb.

"It's all right, it's all right. Please stay calm. Don't allow your mind to wander; just keep breathing." Professor Anna spoke gently in order to soothe the students. "Soon, you will temporarily lose your five physical senses entirely. It should feel much like your existence has completely disappeared from this world. But remember...though it may feel that way, you are still here. In this state, on what foundation does your consciousness and your mind still stand? Where does it exist? Please search carefully for the answer. In the answer, on that foundation...exists your Sphere."

The wind flowed around them. The sound of the blowing tree branches was far away.

The ritual ground was enveloped in stillness.

The students calmed their minds and silently continued their meditation.

Five minutes passed. Then ten.

One hour... Two hours...

But without the five senses, all sense of time was ambiguous.

It was as if time had become infinite and the class was wandering in a void...when suddenly:

"Ah!"

*   *   *

One of the meditating students cried out as if they had come to a realization.

And with that:

"I—I see something…! I see it…!"

"Could this be it…? This feeling…?"

"I—I saw it, too! I felt it!"

"S-so this is where…I exist…?!"

"H-how didn't I ever notice it before?!"

One by one, the students began to call out in surprise.

Seeing their progress, Professor Anna nodded in satisfaction.

"It seems you've begun to grasp it," she said. "Now, those who have felt it, please stand up and open your eyes. Don't worry, the potion will have already worn off by now."

The students did as they were told.

"""""Wh-whoa…"""""

They stood with their eyes wide.

An unimaginable scene was unfolding before them.

"Heh-heh-heh, how is it, everyone?" Professor Anna asked. "Within the Stone Circle, those who have opened their Spheres should now be able to see a physical manifestation of their Sphere and the Spheres of others. What do you think? Visually, it should look something like an orb of light at the center of your body. And you will surely be able to feel everything within that orb. You should feel the sensation of light through your skin, see sound with your eyes, and taste scents. Within that orb, you should be able to clearly understand anything and everything. That is the Sphere. Congratulations. You all have now begun your journey toward becoming mages."

Professor Anna clapped her hands in celebration for the students, some still frozen in surprise and others moved to tears.

"A-amazing… This is a Sphere?!" Randy exclaimed in excitement.

"I did it…! Me, of all people…! Even someone like me…," Annie said with tears of joy.

"Oh-ho, those are some fine Spheres you two have," Serephina remarked.

"Serephina!"

"From what I can tell, each of your Spheres is about five to six meters wide. That's quite good for someone who's only just opened their Sphere. You should be proud."

"D-do you think so…?"

"By the way, for comparison's sake, how big is your Sphere, Serephina?" Randy asked.

"Oh-ho, it would be easier to simply show you rather than explain! Pay close attention! Behold my magnificent Sphere!" Serephina boomed confidently with an exaggerated flourish of her hands.

""""Whoooooaaaaaaa?!""""

Randy, Annie, and the other students shouted in surprise.

"Wh-what's with that Sphere?!"

"I-it's huge! That's gotta be over fifty meters!"

"And its field gives off so much power…!"

"Amazing… She's on a totally different level…"

Serephina was on cloud nine, basking in the praise of her peers.

"Oh-ho-ho. Could this be the effect of the Fool's Elixir?" she said. "I was able to reexamine parts of my Sphere that I had only been able to sense vaguely before, so perhaps that led to it becoming even stronger."

"Heh-heh, I'm not surprised, Serephina. Thank you for showing yours as an example," Professor Anna said with a smile.

"D-dammit… She's a monster!" Alfred, meanwhile, was sourly pushing his glasses back up.

Faced with this crowd of excited students…

Oh crap… I have absolutely no idea what they're talking about.

*   *   *

...Rix had broken into a cold sweat.

In all honesty, Rix was still completely lost.

No matter how much of the potion he used or how much he meditated, he had no clue what this cryptic sensation of the Sphere was supposed to be like. He couldn't see whatever everyone else seemed to be seeing, either.

Unable to participate in the excitement, he felt extremely isolated.

Ummm... Maybe it's just me, but this seems real bad...

Rix didn't fully understand it even after hearing all the explanations, although he did get that it wouldn't be possible to become a mage if he didn't awaken to this mysterious sensation called the Sphere.

And yet he showed no sign of being anywhere close to doing that.

Oh crap, oh crap, oh crap... What do I do...?

Rix was filled with trepidation.

"All right, then! It looks like you've all finished opening your Spheres!" Professor Anna announced. "After becoming aware of the existence of your Sphere and opening it for the first time, you will naturally be able to sense and open your Sphere as you like without relying on potions. With that, I'd like to bring today's class to an end!"

It sounded like Professor Anna was getting ready to conclude the lesson.

This was going to end without Rix having opened his Sphere, which he needed to do in order to become a mage.

This was no time for hesitation.

"U-um..."

Having made up his mind, Rix timidly raised his hand.

"Oh? Is something wrong, Rix?" the professor asked.

"Um, so... This is really hard for me to say, but..."

"What is it?"

"I...haven't opened my Sphere yet... What should I do?"

Silence.

* * *

The excitement from mere moments ago suddenly vanished. All attention turned to Rix.

He had never experienced something so awkward.

"Um...perhaps you didn't get enough of the potion? Why don't you try taking another drop...?" Professor Anna suggested.

"I already used up the whole thing. I don't feel any different at all, though."

"Th-the whole thing?! How are you not dead?!"

Rix showed the now empty bottle to the professor, who was visibly startled.

The crowd went quiet once again.

"Hey, come on, Rix... Cut it out with the bad jokes!"

"Th-that's right! Honestly, it's not even funny!"

Randy and Annie forced smiles as they teased Rix.

"..."

But Rix looked pretty serious.

"U-um... For real?"

"For real. Heh. What should I do?"

Rix shrugged, completely at a loss.

""""Whaaaaaaaat?!"""""

The students went into a frenzy.

"Wait, are you serious?! You literally haven't awakened your Sphere?!" Randy exclaimed.

"You're lying, right?! That can't be true! Wait—what the?!" Serephina cried. "All that slicing you did to the sea monster and launching that idiot Gordon into the wall with your punches...that was just you?! Your own innate abilities?! Not physical enhancement magic or enchantment spells?!"

"Dude, are you even human?! You're not actually a demon or something, are you?!" Randy yelled.

"Whoa, rude!"

Serephina, Randy, and Rix were in an uproar.

"N-no way... Rix..." Annie was looking at Rix with concern.

"M-may I check something?" Professor Anna asked. She walked up to Rix and placed a finger on his forehead.

Then, for a short while, she whispered some sort of chant under her breath.

"...Y-you're right... Rix, your Sphere...isn't open at all. This is quite unusual," she said. "Even those with very little natural inclination to magic should be able to open their Spheres at least a few centimeters..."

The students began to buzz at Anna's statement.

"P-please stay calm, everyone! Calm down!" she urged, trying to settle them as she looked around. "I will deal with Rix's case personally. Now, given the situation, I would like to check once more: Is there anyone else here whose Sphere hasn't opened? If so, please be honest and speak up. This has great bearing on your future at the academy..."

The rest of the students began eyeing each other suspiciously.

Then...

"..."

One person had silently raised their hand.

It was the white-haired girl—Shino.

"What? Y-you too? M-my goodness..."

Professor Anna looked baffled, as if she had seen something she couldn't believe. Shino nodded back silently.

The rest of the students started murmuring to one another once again.

Rix and Shino were widely known to be the scholarship students who had been welcomed into the academy with much fanfare. Thus, their peers were understandably shaken to learn that these two people had yet to open their Spheres.

"I-I've just confirmed it, and yes…both Shino's and Rix's Spheres are completely closed…"

Professor Anna checked Shino's Sphere in the same way she had Rix's, with a troubled expression.

"S-seriously…?! What the hell is going on…?" Randy whispered to Serephina.

"Hmm… To think that the Spheres of the only scholarship students the academy has had in a few years wouldn't open," she whispered back. "It doesn't seem like a coincidence."

The two of them exchanged pained looks.

"Wh-what should we do…? I've never encountered this situation before… And for it to be with the scholarship students… This must be the first time this has happened in the academy's history…," Professor Anna managed to say. "I-in any case, everyone, please keep this to yourselves. I will consult with the academy's leadership to determine what should be our next course of action… I'll end class here. Thank you, and good work today."

The White Class's first lesson at the academy concluded with unresolved turmoil.

"Hmph. So those scholarship students weren't anything special after all," Alfred said loudly enough for the people around him to hear as he headed back to the dormitory.

The other students looked back and forth between Rix and Alfred, as if comparing them, before walking off uncomfortably.

"Ha-ha-ha! Man, I'm in trouble, aren't I…?" Rix sighed and scratched his head, at a loss.

"R-Rix, try not to get discouraged… Professor Anna is a great mage…so I'm sure she'll find some way to help you," Annie told him, doing her best to cheer him up.

Randy and Serephina, however, didn't seem to know what to say.

Rix sensed this awkwardness and looked over at Shino.

"…"

But Shino was the same as usual.

Even in this situation, she looked as disinterested in everything as ever.

She wasn't interested in what was going to happen to her after this, and she didn't care. That was the vibe she was giving off.

"Oh man…"

Becoming a mage and leaving that bloodstained world behind him…

Rix couldn't help but think this dream of his wasn't going to be as easy as he had hoped.

Chapter 4
Threat of Expulsion

"I believe we should expel them at once."

Darwin Streek's voice cut like a knife through the headmaster's office.

Darwin was one of the instructors at the academy, mainly in charge of the magical combat class.

He had long black hair and a gloomy aura, as if his whole body was shrouded in darkness. Only his piercing eyes shone brightly from his visage like daggers.

"We have no need for the incompetent at our noble academy. Rix Frestat and Shino Whytenight should both be expelled immediately, Headmaster," Darwin said as he glared reproachfully at Rix and Shino, who had been summoned to the headmaster's office.

"...Hmm." Headmaster Jake was seated at his desk, with his hands folded before him; he seemed to be deep in thought.

Eeeeek! Oh crap, oh crap, oh crap! Rix thought.

He was trembling with fear like a small animal in the clutches of a hunter.

"..."

Shino, on the other hand, looked entirely disinterested as usual.

Their Spheres couldn't be unlocked. After this discovery, Rix and Shino had been subjected to all kinds of medicinal concoctions under the supervision of many different instructors, over and over, in order to open their Spheres.

They had also been tested with a number of strange magical methods.

But in the end, it was all futile; Rix and Shino's Spheres weren't budging.

"If their Spheres still haven't opened after all we've done, I believe it is certain," said Darwin. "These two do not have the qualities necessary to become mages—that is, unlocked Spheres. In which case, it is only logical that we should expel them, correct?"

"Hmm, you may be right! Unfortunately, that would usually be the case!" Headmaster Jake replied, unbothered.

Rix felt ready to cry.

But—

"However, these two are scholarship students! That means they must possess some kind of extraordinary magical ability! I don't think it's appropriate to run them out of the academy before we figure out what those extraordinary abilities are, do you?!"

"Perhaps there is some kind of issue with the magic tool used to select the students? It is quite old, after all."

Rix blinked in confusion as he watched the back-and-forth between Headmaster Jake and Professor Darwin.

Professor Anna, who was also present, whispered into Rix's ear. "Every year…scholarship students are selected using a special magic tool called the Annals of the One-Horned Goddess."

"'Annals of the One-Horned Goddess'?" Rix repeated.

"Yes. And that tool…intervenes with fate," she added. "The Annals seek out rare magical talents that, without intervention, are destined to be lost without ever standing on the front lines of history, and it brings them forward. The Annals do not tell us the nature of those magical talents, but we use these three years at the academy to investigate them carefully."

So that had been the circumstances behind Rix's selection.

For the first time, Rix learned why a mercenary like him, who'd never had any involvement with magic, had received that special admission invitation to the academy.

But still...Shino and I can't use our Spheres, which are essential in using magic... Maybe that old book thing was wrong after all, Rix thought as he tried to process everything.

"And yet the Annals of the One-Horned Goddess has a long and successful record! Every individual who has been chosen by the book has gone on to become a great mage who will go down in history!" the headmaster boomed. "Bearing this in mind, we cannot simply ignore that it was Rix and Shino the Annals chose on this occasion!"

"Then what are we to do? We've already tried everything we could think of to open their Spheres," said Darwin, who remained cold and emotionless. "And while I've always hated Fools who decide to become mages, I haven't cut any corners. As such, I believe the possibility of their Spheres opening is hopelessly low. And as long as their Spheres remain unopened, the two of them will be unable to keep up in their classes. I think it would be in their best interest to expel them as soon as possible."

The other instructors in attendance seemed to agree. They eyed Rix and Shino sympathetically.

So this is the end, huh? Welp...the dream was nice while it lasted..., thought Rix, sliding into a funk.

"Hmm, in that case, allow me to ask: What do you two wish to do?" Headmaster Jake suddenly said to Rix and Shino.

"Huh?!"

"What do you wish to do going forward? What is your hope?" he asked. "But let's not get too hopeful—in all likelihood, I don't think it will be possible for you! If your Spheres still haven't opened after all that effort, I don't believe you will be able to become mages! However, in the face of the possibility that it may be hopeless or futile... under such uncertainty, would you still dream of being rewarded for your efforts someday and aim to become mages?! Or would you rather make a clean break and give up now and choose to walk a different path?! What, exactly, do you want to do?! I want to hear your honest wishes!"

"…!"

Rix peered deep into his heart.

But he didn't even need to look for the answer—it was right there.

"I…I want to become a mage. I threw away everything I had for that very purpose. I can't give up now."

In response…

"I see! In that case, I will put a *temporary hold* on your expulsion! Please keep striving toward your dream!" Headmaster Jake declared.

Darwin sniffed disapprovingly.

"Huh?! You'll let me off so easily?! You don't need to ask my reasoning or my goal or anything?!" Rix said.

"Ha-ha-ha! No need! Such things are meaningless," Headmaster Jake told him. "Each person's values are different. One person may have a reason that seems ridiculous to another—but if it is genuine to that person, then it is genuine! Accordingly, what is most important is your own will! And you have expressed your will! I need nothing more!"

Next, the headmaster looked at Shino.

"Now, Shino! What shall you do?! What is your will?!" he demanded.

"…"

For a while, Shino continued to sit silently.

Then she finally whispered, "I—"

"I think she feels the same as I do!"

For some reason, Rix reflexively shouted over Shino.

"!"

Ignoring Shino's vaguely surprised expression, Rix continued, "She's always saying how she loves magic! And how she's always aspired to be a mage! So there's no way she'd rather be expelled! She can't give up yet!"

He wasn't really sure why he was yelling this. But he had a feeling that if he didn't say something, Shino might—

"...I want her to stay, too, Headmaster. Please," Professor Anna said, bowing her head. "Shino was one of the students nominated by the Annals of the One-Horned Goddess...so she must possess some fantastic magical ability! I'll take responsibility myself and see to it that she opens her Sphere! So please allow her to stay!"

"Hmm... These two want you to stay, but what do you say, Shino?" Headmaster Jake looked back to Shino.

For a while, her silence continued, and her blank gaze wandered.

Then finally, she breathed a sigh as if she had at last reached a decision.

"...I...want to become a mage, too," she said.

After the conversation was over, Rix and Shino left the headmaster's office.

When they exited the school building, the sky was burning with the light of the setting sun. The castle-like school building, its soaring towers, and the vast courtyard were all dyed red and gold.

Somehow or another, Rix and Shino ended up walking through the school grounds together toward the White Class's dormitory.

"Stay out of it," Shino said out of nowhere.

This girl, who was usually so expressionless, now sounded slightly angry and resentful.

"I knew it. So you were going to let yourself get expelled? I had a feeling," said Rix.

"If you knew, then why did you butt in? It was none of your business."

"Hmm… Honestly, even I'm not quite sure why…" Rix scratched his head as he tried to explain. "It's like…I just had a feeling you were thinking that you didn't really want to leave the academy."

"…!"

At that moment, Shino's expression clearly wavered.

Then she muttered in frustration, "…On what grounds?"

"Just a feeling. And I'm usually right. Thanks to that, I've survived this long."

Shino grew unusually enraged, glaring at Rix as if he were a pile of garbage.

"Gross! You're seriously disgusting! What's *with* you?!"

"Oof! Urgh! Ack! O-ow… That hurts so bad… Worse than any wound I've had on the battlefield…!" Rix groaned. "But…heh-heh… What a shame. Just when I was finally starting to feel better… Urgh!"

"You're vile…" Shino was visibly disgusted.

"By the way, I have proof. For some reason or another, you made the effort to come to this faraway academy, and in the end, you chose to stay," said Rix. "If you really, truly wanted to quit, you wouldn't have done that, right?"

"Hmph. You don't understand anything. It just would have been more trouble to withdraw. I don't have anything else to do, so I figured I might as well stay. It was the path of least resistance… Don't get the wrong idea."

"I—I see…"

"Ugh, what rotten luck, getting involved with a pervert like you. Makes me want to puke."

"Ah, what a treat, more insults. Thank you so much."

Shino shot Rix a look of utter disgust before turning away.

Then she whispered, "…Hmph. You're…just like *him*."

"Hmm?" Rix peered at Shino's face, but she ignored him.

He was pretty sure she wasn't going to elaborate on what she'd meant by that whisper any time soon.

So he put it out of his mind for now.

"Anyway, let's both do our best here, starting tomorrow! Right, Shino?"

"…Be quiet. Don't get all chummy with me. It's gross."

Then the White Class dormitory, which looked like some kind of noble's mansion, came into view.

And—

"Heeey! Rix! Shino!"

"How was it?! I mean…do you get to stay?!"

—Randy, Annie, and Serephina, who had been waiting for the pair, ran toward them with worried looks on their faces.

Chapter 5
Days at the Academy

And so, while the journey ahead didn't look like it was going to be easy, Rix started off his new life at Estoria Academy of Magic.

The first class of the day was physical enhancement magic.

Rix and the rest of the White Class gathered at a magic training ground behind the school building—a large oval-shaped dirt field surrounded by a magic barrier.

In general, classes at Estoria Academy of Magic were separated by color, each under the supervision of an instructor.

All these instructors were Rank Two Estoria Certified Mages or higher and were accomplished in their own rights.

"Aaahhh... So sleepy... I'm exhausted... This sucks... Even breathing is a pain... If only the world would just end..."

However, the instructor who appeared before the White Class was extremely shabby.

He looked to be about in his late twenties. He was tall and lanky, like a bean sprout, with raggedy gray hair and eyes like a dead fish, and he wore a threadbare, wrinkly black robe.

There were deep, dark circles under his eyes. His face was covered in stubble, and he had a cigarette in his mouth.

He was like the living embodiment of sloppiness, laziness, drowsiness, and apathy all rolled into one.

"Ugh…I'm Crawford Rockwell," the man began. "It's a pain, but for the record, I'm a Rank Two Estoria Certified Mage, and I'll be your instructor. Nice to meet you. Anyway, not like I really want to, but it's time to start the class… I guess it is my job, after all…"

Professor Crawford announced this while puffing a billow of purple smoke into the air from his cigarette.

At the same time, the bell signaling the beginning of the class period rang out across the school grounds.

The students were clearly wondering, *Is this guy okay?* But they tried to put their uncertainties aside as class began.

"Uh, what class is this again? Oh yeah, I'm in charge of physical enhancement magic… It's, you know. Basics of the basics. Superbasics of magic. The foundation of all magic. Like, if you can't do physical enhancement magic to a certain extent, you won't be able to do anything else. Ugh, what a pain."

Crawford kept puffing away at his cigarette.

"You've all opened your Spheres, yes? Oh…right, I guess some of you haven't yet…" He glanced over at Rix and Shino. "Well, whatever. I'm gonna explain to everyone regardless. First off, you all know how within the bounds of your Sphere, you're omnipotent, right? Within those bounds, you can perceive everything and control all phenomena freely. That's basically what magic is. So a question for you. Raise your hand if you know the answer. Within the bounds of your Sphere, what is the thing you have the most ability to control and manipulate?"

After Crawford asked the question, he must have thought it was too much of a pain to call on anyone, so he just answered it. "That's right, your*self*. Good answer. Have a gold star."

Serephina, Alfred, Annie, and a few other students who had been raising their hands confidently now turned red and awkwardly lowered their hands.

"Humans have this pain of a biomagnetic spiritual power we call magnetite," said Crawford. "It's a stupid fundamental life energy that arises from all your stupid emotions—joy, anger, sadness, fear—as well as a result of all the stupid activities in your daily life. Mages also call this mana. Though explaining it's a pain."

The students were starting to think, *This guy just wants to say "stupid," "dumb," and "pain" as much as possible, doesn't he?*

"Ordinary people who haven't opened their Spheres aren't able to sense this spiritual energy, or mana. But you are all mages with open Spheres. And mages are omnipotent within their Spheres," Crawford went on. "Obviously, that means you can grasp the sensation of that stupid mana stuff. And while the necessary training is a pain, eventually you can manipulate it like an extension of your body. Magic, in itself, is the supernatural phenomenon of taking that stupid mana as an energy source and using it as a driving force within your Sphere.

"Then that means it's possible to strengthen your physical abilities, sharpen your vision and reflexes, and enhance your self-healing abilities by pouring mana into the self at the core of your Sphere, right? That's what we call physical enhancement magic. The basis of all other magic. I know it's a pain, but in this class, we're gonna focus on training in that basic physical enhancement magic over and over.

"What's even more of a pain: We're gonna work on increasing your mana, expanding and strengthening your Sphere, and other kinds of spiritual ability training like that, too. Think of it like an athlete building up their basic fitness.

"It may be a huge pain, but you'll need to do your best to keep up if you want to call yourself a mage." Crawford sleepily gazed at the students. "Honestly, what you all have to do in this class is simple. Move your body while pouring mana into it, meditate while manipulating your Sphere... I guess I'll make up a training schedule later that accounts for people's individual levels. What a pain.

"Anyway, in today's physical enhancement magic class, I wanted you to understand the basic concept and how it works...and it just so happens we've got a good example for comparison here with us."

Crawford called on a few students.

"Alfred. Your Sphere is open, and you've got some proficiency with using it. And Rix. Your Sphere isn't open yet. I know it's a pain, but please come stand in front of the class."

The two boys got up, cocking their heads in confusion.

Crawford continued speaking as the students started to mumble among themselves.

"Let me first say this: There is absolutely no way for an ordinary person who hasn't opened their Sphere to win in a physical competition against a mage who has opened their Sphere," Crawford told the class. "That's because a proficient mage can use physical enhancement magic just as easily as they breathe. I want you all to witness firsthand how much of a difference this physical enhancement magic can make in a mage compared to an ordinary person. You two. I know it's a pain, but I want you to race to that pole over there. No need to hold back. Give it all the power you've got."

"W-wait just a second, Professor Crawford!"

"Yeah, hold on! This is a bit much, isn't it?"

Annie and Randy began to shout.

"Allow me to dissent as well, Professor," Serephina offered. "You cannot allow such an act of public humiliation, for the sake of the person's honor!"

"Public humiliation? ...I guess I can't help it if you all feel that way. What a pain." Crawford scratched his head awkwardly. "Still...I know it sounds dumb, but you've really got to see it to believe it. If you can just see the obvious difference that exists between ordinary people and mages, I think you'll want to put more effort into this stupid class going forward, won't you? Rix, I'm sorry for making you play such a crappy role, but...you don't mind, do you?"

"Oh, I'm totally fine with it! You just want us to run as fast as we can to that pole and back, right?" said Rix. "Hmm, looks like it's around two hundred meters…"

Rix started leisurely stretching his legs in preparation for the race.

"H-hey! Rix!" Randy cried. "I said wait a second!"

"Professor, please, can you call off the race?!" Serephina urged.

The two of them kept trying to put a stop to things.

"Ha-ha-ha-ha-ha! How touching that you're so concerned for your friend!" Alfred sneered. "You've only just met, but you sure are close already, huh?! You really don't want Rix to embarrass himself in front of us that badly?"

"No, that's not it! That's not the concern here!" said Randy.

"Indeed! Alfred, don't go along with this stupid race!" added Serephina.

"Hmph! As if!" Alfred shot a hateful look at Rix. "I'll tell you straight up, Rix… I never liked you, right from the start."

"Huh? Me?"

"Yeah, you! Magic is supposed to be a special right of the privileged noble class! In the first place, I hate it when commoners think they can use that pathetic potion to become mages. But even you, some common idiot from who knows where, gets to be a scholarship student? Ha! And you can't even open your Sphere. You're a failure!"

Alfred smirked faintly as he declared this in front of everyone.

"I'll crush you, Rix," he said. "I'll show everyone how different we really are. You'd better get ready for this."

"S-stop, Alfreeeeeeed! Please, don't do iiiiiiiiiiiit!" Randy screamed, clutching his head.

"He's right! Listen to him! Oh goodness… This poor boy! I can't watch…" Serephina held back tears.

"Ha-ha-ha-ha-ha! Rix, you may have zero ability as a mage, but you clearly know how to work some magic with your words! Maybe you should become a professional swindler!"

"Huh, so like being a wizard but using only words…," said Rix. "That's a good way to put it!"

"""No it's not!""" Randy, Annie, and Serephina cried simultaneously.

"…What a pain. Can we just start the race already?" Crawford said as he wearily exhaled a cloud of purple smoke.

"All right, I know it's a pain, but…on your mark, get set, go…"

Following a lazy starting call from Crawford, Rix and Alfred started running.

And off to a perfect start, taking the lead was…Alfred.

"…Hmph!"

In a flash, he had used his Sphere to pour mana throughout his entire body, concentrating his physical enhancement magic on strengthening his legs.

He had probably already had quite a bit of training in this at home.

With not a single second of hesitation in the flow of his mana, his physical enhancement magic was almost a perfect example.

His body continued to explosively accelerate as he flew like an arrow toward the pole they had set as the race's goal.

My body feels as light as a feather… And lately, my mana's been in top condition! Alfred thought as everything in his field of vision flew behind him in a torrent.

But having also seamlessly enhanced his vision and reflexes, he didn't lose control over his body, even at this speed.

Then his classmates' astonished cries started to reach his ears.

"N-no way…!"

"Is he for real?!"

"Is there supposed to be this big a difference between an ordinary person and a mage?!"

Alfred grinned.

Then without letting up, he ruthlessly accelerated even more.

Alfred flew past the goal like a gale—

—but Rix was already there waiting for him.

"Whaaaaaaaaaaaaaaaaaaaaaaat?!"

*   *   *

Screeeeech—! Rix had come skidding to a halt next to the pole and was already catching his breath as Alfred fell and rolled past him.

"Good race, Alfred. Let's do it again sometime."

Cheerfully and pleasantly, Rix extended his hand to Alfred.

"Huh?! Whaaaat?! Huuuuuh?! What just happened?!" Alfred hollered. "How did you get here before me?! Whaaaaaaaaat?!"

Still collapsed on the ground, Alfred looked up at Rix and flew into a panic.

"Seems like he beat him by quite a gap, too..."

"What does this mean...?"

"Huh? Wait, which one of them hasn't opened their Sphere? Alfred?"

The speculating students were lost in confusion.

"That's why we were trying to tell you..."

"A prayer for the courageous souls of the fallen..."

"Ah-ha-ha-ha..."

Randy, Serephina, and Annie offered their exasperated condolences.

Crawford had been watching Rix and Alfred's race from afar.

"...Hmm. Hrmmm..."

He sank into thought for a little while, puffing out purple smoke.

Then, finally...

"So there you have it. There you can see the stark and decisive difference in the physical abilities of an ordinary person and a mage," Crawford remarked. "Now let's move right along to working on your own physical enhancement magic. Are you ready?"

As if nothing unusual had happened, he nonchalantly moved on to the next point on the agenda.

Let me guess... It was too much of a pain for him.

That's what all the students were thinking.

———————

"Aaahhh, I'm beat…," Randy muttered after the first period's physical enhancement magic class was over. He and the others were in the classroom for their next period, waiting for it to start.

"That was my first time trying physical enhancement magic…but I feel like my mind is more exhausted than my body…or like my spirit is exhausted…," said Randy.

"Yeah…now I really get what people mean when they say their Sphere is exhausted…," Annie agreed with a strained smile.

"That's the sensation of your mana being used up. It is a strange feeling when you first experience it," Serephina added.

Rix stared happily at his palms. "I see… So that's what this feeling is. Like I've worked up a good sweat…"

"That's definitely not what we're feeling," Randy quipped. "But man, we practiced for a whole hour and a half, and all I could do was manage to run a little faster than before."

"I—I couldn't even do that… I wonder if I'll be okay…," said Annie.

"Worry not," Serephina told her. "Everyone has trouble at the start."

"That's right! If you keep practicing, soon you'll be able to catch up with me!" said Rix.

"No way."

"Don't think so."

"No chance."

"Rix, are you seriously even human?" Randy asked. "I'm starting to have my doubts…"

As the group was chatting, the bell signaling the start of class rang, and the instructor walked in.

"Let's begin. Welcome to black magic class."

The person who entered was a beautiful woman of indeterminate age. Her purple hair was fastened in an updo, and her eyes were the color of blood. Her skin was pale white, like wax.

Her appearance was that of a bewitching mature woman, a fresh and vibrant youth, and a budding young girl, all at once.

And of course, she was wearing the black robes of a full-fledged mage.

"My name is Arca Claudia, Estoria Certified Mage, Rank One."

She calmly introduced herself from where she stood at the head of the class.

"In short, that means I belong to the highest class of mages in this world. So please rest assured that I am more than qualified to teach and guide you nascent mages."

There were clearly many students in the class who already knew Arca's name.

Throughout the classroom, students started to whisper things like "To think we'll be taught by *the* Arca Claudia!" and "We're so lucky!"

"But really...how old do you figure she is?" Rix whispered to Randy.

"Who knows? Rumor has it she's actually a vampire who's lived over a hundred years."

"Ahem."

They were pretty sure there was no way she had heard them, but Arca cleared her throat to regain the class's attention.

"You have all opened your Spheres, commenced training in physical enhancement magic, and have begun to vainly believe you have come closer to understanding the essence of magic. But you are wrong," Arca began. "Except perhaps a few of you students of high stature who have already begun training before attending the academy, surely none of you can even satisfactorily kindle a fire within the omnipotent bounds of your own Sphere. And why is that? Because you do not yet know *how to kindle a fire.*"

Ignoring the noisy students around her, Arca continued.

"To be sure, within your own Sphere, you are all omnipotent. However, you are not *omniscient.* Why a fire kindles, why lightning forms, by what logic time and space exist...you know none of these things. You are the very essence of ignorant Fools. It goes without saying that one cannot control knowledge that one does not know, nor laws and reason one doesn't understand.

"Unlike physical enhancement magic, which relies on knowing oneself through one's Sphere, one must be *omniscient* in order to manipulate external phenomena with *omnipotence*. The path to that omniscience...that fragment of omniscient omnipotence that is to know the very truth of this world...that shred of truth that serves as a guidepost to the free exercise of magic... is knowledge. Law and reason. This is what you will learn in the form of what we call magic formulas over the next three years. By using your own magic within the omnipotent Sphere according to these magic formulas, the very marrow of our knowledge, you shall create your own first magical work."

All around the classroom, the students voiced their wonder at Arca's explanation.

"Today's class will be split into a first half and a second half," she added. "In the first half, you will learn the first spell that all new students learn, the most common fire spell: Ember. I will teach you all the magic formula for this spell. Then in the second half, we will go out to the training grounds and practice the actual execution of that Ember spell. Understood?"

And with that, Professor Arca began her instruction.

"Black magic investigates the physical and scientific logic of this world: heat and energy, the motion of objects, sound, electricity and magnetism, elements and their properties, light and waves, gravity, time and space...and so on," the professor explained. "Black magic seeks the truths of this world—omniscient omnipotence—through the mastery of its fundamental laws. Hence, there is a precise, subtle, and rational chemistry underlying the magic formulas of black magic. Are we good thus far, everyone? Please do your utmost to *understand* the concepts learned in this class. There's no place for rote memorization and the like when it comes to using magic."

Prefacing thus, Professor Arca drew a pentagram-shaped geometric figure on the blackboard and added mathematical formulas and instructions to each part of the figure.

The magic formula itself looked to be a schematic diagram that included a rough sketch of the world, the flow of power behind a particular phenomenon, the natural laws at the phenomenon's root, and the mathematical function and output calculation for the mana needed to manipulate the phenomenon.

At first, the students had no idea what the magic formula meant, but Professor Arca carefully explained the meaning of each aspect of the formula one by one.

What is the phenomenon of a fire starting in the first place?

What of the flow of energy behind the event and the movement of the elements that make up this world? How does one convert mana, a spiritual energy, into heat, a physical energy? And how does one do it efficiently?

Arca explained these difficult theories in a simple and concise manner, using language anyone could understand, and without being overly pretentious.

She even accounted for taking extra care in the sections that she knew would be particularly difficult for beginner mages; it was a perfect explanation.

And by the time the first half of the class was reaching its end, the students had understood the concept. They fundamentally understood the phenomenon of a fire starting in this world.

And they didn't simply understand it logically. They understood with their souls.

"I—I get it now..."

"So this is why Professor Arca's so famous..."

"They don't call her the Obsidian Sage for nothing..."

After hearing the professor's explanation, students around the room began to whisper.

"Hmm... Flame magic is supposed to be my specialty, but this made me realize my understanding is still too shallow," Serephina noted, looking deeply impressed.

"So even you feel that way, Serephina…" Annie widened her eyes in surprise.

Meanwhile, Randy started excitedly talking to Rix, who was next to him.

"Professor Arca's lectures are difficult, but she makes it so easy to understand, right?!"

"Yeah. She made it really easy to understand that I have no idea what she's talking about. She's incredible…" Rix seemed deeply moved.

"Are you serious right now…?" Randy stared at him suspiciously.

Among the students who were so taken with Arca's lesson…

"…Hmph."

…only one—Shino—looked bored. She leaned her head on her hand and stared out the window.

"All right now, everyone. Let's hurry over to the magic training grounds," said Arca. "It's time to put what you've learned about the Ember spell into practice."

———————

"I bring forth a stone of flame!"

The students' shouts echoed over the magic training grounds, where a number of round targets were lined up.

The students stood some distance away and expanded their Spheres.

With their shouts, their mana flowed through their Spheres in accordance with the magic formula they'd just learned.

And then—

"Whoa?!"

—a small ball of fire like a stone appeared and flew out from each student's fingertips.

The balls of fire flew toward the targets and burned them.

"Wow! I did it! I really did it?!"

Randy's eyes widened; he was incredulous.

Around him, other students were succeeding in casting their first spell as well.

"The incantation you are now shouting is a simplified version of the contents of the magic formula required in order to exercise the spell."

As the students practiced, Arca continued her explanation.

"Words have power, akin to their own spirit, which deeply affects one's inner world when uttered. By reciting these incantations, it becomes easier for your mana to flow according to the magic formula. However, there is no need to worry about sticking exactly to existing incantations. As long as it allows your mana to flow more easily, any word will do. And ultimately…"

Suddenly, Arca snapped her fingers.

A dozen small flames appeared above her head, and she sent them flying toward the targets. Every single one struck its target dead center, and the targets all simultaneously went up in flames.

It was clear that Arca's Ember was on an entirely different level in heat and firepower compared with the students' spells.

As the students gasped in amazement, Arca continued without a single note of pride in her voice.

"Chantless spellcasting. Deepen your understanding and mastery of magic formulas, and the spell takes on a natural reason of your own creation. To be able to have your mana flow smoothly and efficiently according to the magic formula without reciting an incantation… That is the goal you all should be striving for."

The apparent, stark difference in Arca's power rendered the students speechless.

"Hmm, simply remarkable. While I'm able to use the same chantless spellcasting, the quality of Arca's flames is like solid ice, while mine are like lukewarm water. I'm not even close to that level of power and precision…"

Serephina was astounded.

"Damn. So this is the power of one of the world's most prestigious mages." For some reason, Alfred started talking to Rix. "I hope I can reach that level someday... Don't you feel the same, Rix?"

"..."

"Oh, right, my bad. That's impossible for you, isn't it? You don't even have a Sphere. It's totally out of the question for you to get that good... Heh-heh-heh..."

Alfred laughed scornfully.

Immediately, the atmosphere started turning sour.

"You there, stop the chitchat. Would you like some points taken off your grade?"

Unable to abide the distraction, Arca gave Alfred a warning.

"That's actually not true at all, Alfred," Rix replied. "I bet I can manage something around that level."

""""What?!"""""

His classmates were shocked.

"...Oh, really?" Arca looked at Rix with interest.

"Listen, you... Don't go running your mouth about things you aren't able to back up!" Annoyed by Rix's complacency, Alfred began calling him out. "You think you can pull off something superhuman like that, when you don't even have a Sphere?! That's just insulting to the professor, no matter how you look at it!"

Rix was persistently irreverent. "No, really, I can. It's actually pretty simple. I mean...it'll take a bit more time than Professor Arca's spell did, but..."

"Interesting. Please, go ahead and try." Professor Arca started encouraging him out of genuine interest. "Rix, I know you haven't opened your Sphere yet. As a mage, I am truly interested in how you expect to replicate what I have just done."

"P-Professor! He's just making rash remarks; don't take him seriously!"

"Alfred. One absolutely necessary quality of a mage is the flexibility in thinking that allows them to question existing common sense and fixed ideas. For that very reason: Please go ahead, Rix. If you are to boast so boldly before me, please don't leave me disappointed."

"I've got this, Professor. All right, one moment, please…"

Rix ran toward the forest outside the magic training grounds at an amazing speed…and when he finally returned, he was carrying a bunch of dead branches in his arms.

The students began to buzz.

Alfred and Professor Arca blinked at him, wondering what he could be up to.

Don't tell me…

No way…

He can't be…

Randy, Annie, and Serephina already had a bad feeling.

And then Rix got to work.

"*I bring forth a stone of flaaaaame!*" he shouted with a furious look on his face, drilling a dead branch into some wood chips he had placed on the ground.

Scritch, scritch, scritch, scritch! The deafening sound of wood rubbing against wood reverberated around them.

"Ah-ha-ha-ha-ha! Are you stupid? There's no way you can make a fire like tha—"

Poof!

"A fire?!"

Alfred's eyes looked like they were about to pop out of his head.

Arca was looking dumbfounded, herself.

"*I bring forth, a stone of flaaame! I bring forth! A stone of flaaaaaaame!!*"

Rix used this method to light each branch and make them into torches.

Soon enough, he had about a dozen of these torches.

He then picked them up and stood in front of the targets.

"*I! Bring forth! A stone! Of flaaaaaaaaaaaaaaaaame!*"

*   *   *

Using every fiber of his being, he flung the bundle of torches at the targets.

Each torch flew toward its target with unparalleled accuracy.

Crack!

All the targets were simultaneously demolished.

"""""   """""
....

The students' jaws fell to the floor.

"See, it's just like Professor Arca said." Having completed his task, Rix smiled brightly. "Words are power, with their own spirit!"

"I'm pretty sure this isn't what she meant," Randy quipped back, right on schedule.

"...Rix." Arca turned to face Rix with an inscrutable expression.

"Eep?! P-please, Professor, don't be angry with him!"

"This guy, he's just an idiot! I swear, he's just a harmless, extreme dumbass!"

"I'll be sure to punish him severely myself, so please, spare him this time!"

Annie, Randy, and Serephina rushed to cover for their friend, but it was already too late.

Arca stood before Rix and slowly raised her hands.

"Magnificent."

With an uncharacteristically tender expression, she placed her hands gently on Rix's shoulders.

"I see... So this method exists, too. Thanks to you, I was able to break down another of my fixed ideas about common sense, even at my age. I thank you."

"Professor...I think you'd better keep that common sense intact...," Randy urged, rounding off the day's black magic class.

———————

"Good day, everyone. My name is Ray Doctrice. I am the instructor in charge of the white magic class. Pleased to make your acquaintance."

It was time for white magic class.

The person who appeared in the classroom before the students of the White Class was a man with bright blond hair and blue eyes.

With his silky hair, intelligent yet gentle eyes, and exquisitely well-featured and sweet face, he was a stunningly beautiful young man. The moment he appeared, the female students squealed.

"If black magic is said to deal with the outside world—that is, physical laws and energies—then white magic is an inquiry of the inner world—the body and spirit, the mysteries of life, and the very existence of living things," Ray began. "At times, it heals the bodies of the wounded, at times changes or transforms the body itself, and yet other times it deludes the hearts of others, produces illusions before them, or even curses their existence itself. White magic has its own dangerous side that is different from that of black magic. I ask that you please take care to never abuse it."

""""Yes, Professor! ♥"""""

Ray was smiling gently, and all the girls in the room—save for Annie, Serephina, and Shino—clasped their hands together, responding in unison.

"Tch, this is why I hate handsome men…"

"Seriously, Randy! Does this guy have no shame?! All handsome men should just die!"

"Yeah, exactly! …Though I hate myself a little for having to agree with you on this one thing."

Ray got started, paying no mind to the two idiotic boys.

Today, he would be teaching the magic formula for the Sleep spell. Apparently, it was a foundational spell in mind-control magic that forced the target into a state of sleep.

Ray's class was just as easy to understand as Arca's had been, but the fact that the female students squealed at Ray's each and every move seemed to be gradually annoying and stressing out the male students.

"Now let's give this spell a try. Please cast Sleep on each other per my instructions, taking turns with the person next to you," said Ray.

The male students' struggle was over, and they could move on to actually practicing magic.

"But don't worry," Ray assured the class. "I'll use another spell to immediately wake any students who fall asleep."

""""Aaah! I want to be gently woken up by Professor Raaaay! ♥"""""

""""Tch! Ugh! Grrrrr!"""""

The students, a whirlwind of love and hate, moved on to spell practice.

"*Close thine eyes and tranquility find!* ...How was that? Did it work?"

"Um...? Sorry, Randy. I don't feel any different...," said Annie.

"O-oh, okay... Dammit, this is harder than I thought. When you cast it on me, I fell right to sleep..."

"Grr... White magic has never been my strong point... Annie, can you teach me the trick to it...?"

Most of the students were already having trouble with this first spell. Annie was the only one who had been successful.

"Everyone, there's no need to rush. Compared to black magic, even white magic of the same level is considered much more difficult. Black magic manipulates the outside world, which does not have its own free will, while white magic takes as its subject individuals with their own free will, who can resist."

Ray walked around the room observing the students and trying to reassure them.

Then:

"Hey, Rix. Let's do this: I'll cast Sleep on you, then you on me."

With no sign of changing his tune even after the last incident, Alfred came at Rix with another challenge.

"You're participating in this class, too...which means you have to practice like everyone else, right?" said Alfred. "Let's see who can put the other person into a deeper sleep. You won't try to run away, will you?"

If Rix took him up on it, Alfred would show him no mercy; if he didn't take him up on it, he'd be made into a coward... Regardless, Alfred was clearly scheming to embarrass Rix in front of the entire class.

Nonetheless...

"A challenge? Sure, sounds good. Let's do it."

Rix casually accepted without a second thought.

Hmph, what an idiot. Little does he know that white magic is my forte. My Sleep spell is at a totally different level than even Annie's. And there's no way someone without a Sphere can beat me! Alfred gloated to himself.

"All right, then I'll start," he said. "Here I go! *Close thine eyes and tranquility find!*"

The next instant, Rix became engulfed in the mana that shot from Alfred's fingertips.

"—?!"

Rix was assaulted by an overwhelming sleepiness, and his consciousness began to fade. He was bound to collapse at any moment... and just when it looked like he was about to fall over—

Stab! Gush!

—Rix had pulled a knife seemingly out of nowhere and stabbed it into his own thigh.

And naturally, a huge fountain of blood started gushing out of the wound like a horror show.

"Oof... Nice. Now I'm wide awake."

"Whoaaaaaaaaaaa?!"

"Eeeeeeeeeeeek!!"

Immediately, the classroom flew into a panic.

"You're good, Alfred," said Rix. "But look—I resisted."

"What the—?! What are you doing?! Are you stupid?! Did you need to go that far?!"

Alfred shrank away from Rix, who was grinning boldly.

"I can't hold back when I'm faced with a challenge. Now it's my turn…!"

Alfred was retreating in fear, when suddenly, Rix disappeared.

"What?!"

Before Alfred realized what was happening, Rix appeared behind him and had the boy in a chokehold.

"Eek?! Wh-what do you think you're—?!"

"*Close thine eyes and tranquility fiiiiiiiind!*" Rix screamed as he applied intense pressure to Alfred's neck.

Slump… In an instant, Alfred lost consciousness.

"So this is the Sleep spell, huh? I see… Professor Ray was right; it's a dangerous power that shouldn't be abused… I'll have to be careful."

Rix admonished himself as he looked down at Alfred, who was foaming at the mouth with his eyes rolled back.

"I take my eyes off you for one second, and this happens…," Randy said with a sigh.

"Ah-ha-ha-ha…"

Annie laughed nervously, and Professor Ray rushed over to administer a healing spell.

After one thing and another…Rix's life at the academy went on, with no one ever really knowing what might happen next.

He solved everything by force, relying on his overwhelming physical abilities.

It was pretty much the exact opposite of what a mage should be— that is, walking the path of magic that manipulated the world's delicate laws and logic.

————————

Some days later during lunch break, in the luxurious student dining hall…

"At first, I wasn't sure how it would turn out, but I think I'm doing a pretty good job keeping up with classes!" Rix said cheerfully.

"Uh, no. You're definitely not."

As usual, Randy shot Rix down.

Rix and the others were sitting at the same long table where they usually sat. They had all lined up with their respective meals they had ordered and were in the middle of eating.

"What do you mean, Randy? So far, I've been able to accomplish every assignment the professors have thrown at me, haven't I?"

"Yeah, sure. You're finishing the assignments, but your methods are fundamentally different…"

Randy sighed and brought a spoonful of potato soup to his mouth. Rix was gnawing on some rye bread.

"But I wonder… Indeed, if Rix keeps on going like this, will he be able to become a mage?" Serephina asked as she neatly sliced some roast beef.

"Unfortunately, I think it'll be difficult…," Annie replied hesitantly and poked at her herring pie. "When it comes to the credit examination at the end of the semester, there's really no getting around the requirement to actually use magic… And I don't think there are any instructors who will be convinced by Rix's usual methods…"

"I guess not. And he won't be able to earn enough credits through classroom learning without practical skill." Randy scratched his head, at a loss.

"Isn't there some way I can become a mage, even if I can't use magic?" Rix asked, dead serious.

"What the hell do you think you're saying?"

"Urgh…so it's hopeless as long as my Sphere isn't open…?! In which case, it's only a matter of time before I get expelled…! Please, everyone…don't forget me… Never forget there once was a man named Rix Frestat at this academy…!"

"As if we could forget," Randy quipped, sighing at Rix for what felt like the umpteenth time. "No chance, unless someone goes into my brain and erases my memories."

"Precisely," Serephina agreed.

"Have you made any progress with opening your Sphere anyway? If I remember right, you and Shino have been getting special instruction from Professor Anna after school," Randy added before bringing a fork full of beans simmered with tomato to his mouth.

Peeking off to the side, some distance away, Rix could see Shino eating all alone at another table.

"Beats me! Our Spheres show no signs of opening!" Rix said, unconcerned.

"I—I see... I wonder what could be so different between us...? Even I didn't have any real trouble with mine...," Randy replied awkwardly.

Annie changed the subject. "But you know...Professor Anna is such a good teacher."

"How do you mean?"

"Well, for her to give you and Shino extra instruction after class every day, so patiently and earnestly... She has her own classes and research to worry about, and I don't think just anyone would do that for someone else."

"Oh, yeah, I guess so..." was Rix's noncommittal reply.

"What's wrong? You're downright mumbling... Did something happen with her?" Serephina asked him.

"No, it's nothing. Probably just my imagination. Argh, what should I do? If my Sphere never opens, then..."

"Worry not. Even if you can't become a wizard, with your physical ability, you'll find some way to make your living in the future. Perhaps as a mercenary," said Serephina. "If you like, I'll even hire you as a mercenary! What do you say?"

"No way."

"You so flatly refuse?! Do you hate me that much?!"

Serephina despaired at Rix's answer, her eyes filling with tears. Then—

* * *

"Hmph… You four are awfully chummy as usual. Licking each other's wounds, are you?"

Suddenly, someone had started badmouthing Rix and the others.

When they turned around, they saw Alfred standing there.

"Well, I guess I should expect as much from some common folk playing at becoming mages. You have no serious principles nor convictions about learning magic. You think of magic as nothing but a tool for your own self-fulfillment," Alfred scoffed. "The shallowness of commoners never ceases to amaze me."

"What did you say…?!"

Unable to ignore the insult, Randy stood up and glared at Alfred.

"What? It's the truth, no? And anyway…you're actually happy, aren't you? Now that there's someone even lower than you? That's the only reason you're friends with an ordinary person like Rix, isn't it?"

Not backing down, Alfred glared at Randy.

"What?! I'll make you regret saying that!"

Randy was growing more indignant, but Alfred ignored him and looked over at Rix.

"Rix…I heard all about you. It seems you're actually quite the swordsman, huh? They say you even took down a sea monster with nothing but your sword."

"…"

"I'll have to give you that one. Quite amazing. Yes, truly spectacular. Good boy, good boy. There can't be many humans in this wide world who could take down a sea monster without magic. And yet…what a shame. They say a swordsman can never win against a mage."

Randy and Annie gasped at Alfred's scornful words.

"Hmph, based on your reactions…even you know enough about magic now to understand what I'm saying," Alfred continued. "That's right. No matter how much a swordsman hones their skills, they can't hope to win against even the lowest-level mage. After all, the best a plain old swordsman can do is kill other humans or cut down some lowly monster… And that's an undeniable truth. You may have faked your way through classes this far with your idiotic ideas and your raw strength, but if you and I were to have a real magical duel…you definitely wouldn't be able to win. Actually, it should already be difficult for you to win even against Randy or Annie. Magical combat class will be starting soon…and I'm quite looking forward to it, Rix."

Alfred looked down at Rix with a smug, triumphant smile.

"Zzz…"

But Rix had conked out, with a piece of bread still hanging out of his mouth.

"How dare you fall asleep when I'm talking to you?! Honestly, you never fail to find some way to tick me off!" Alfred howled, grabbing Rix by his lapels and shaking him awake.

"I-I'm really sorry… Your whole spiel was dragging on so long…"

"Hmph! Well, whatever. Just you wait and see; once we're in magical combat training…I'll make sure you understand what they mean when they say a swordsman can never win against a mage. I can imagine it now—you'll be begging at my feet for mercy when I'm done with you. Ah-ha-ha-ha-ha!"

Having finally said his piece, Alfred turned and left.

"Geez…what a jerk," Randy spat.

"Indeed. He's rotten to the core," Serephina muttered.

Annie, meanwhile, did her best to console their friend. "Try not to pay him too much mind, Rix… I'm sure you'll open your Sphere soon enough."

But Rix had noticed that no one had tried to challenge what Alfred had said—that a swordsman can never win against a mage.

"A swordsman can never win against a mage," huh…?

What could that even mean?

Rix thought it over as he gnawed on his bread.

Before long, the bell signaling the end of lunch break rang out across the school grounds.

Chapter 6
Magical Combat Training

One month had passed since the new students had entered the academy.

While there was a difference in ability between individuals, everyone was slowly becoming able to use their magic. Soon, they were notified that the previously restricted magical combat class would soon begin.

And now the day of the first class was upon them.

"I suppose many of you already know me, but my name is Darwin Streek. I'm in charge of the academy's magical combat class. And by the way, I am a Grand Master of Magic with the qualification of Rank One Estoria Certified Mage. The difference in magical abilities between us is worlds apart. Understood? That means do not make me angry if you value your life, you dullards."

Right from the start, Professor Darwin's foreboding introduction and his intense glare made the students tremble.

The class was held in a magic training ground in the basement of the academy.

The students were lined up in an orderly fashion in the center of the large circular field.

Typically, magical combat lessons were conducted together with two classes, but all three—the White Class, the Blue Class, and the Red Class—were present to commemorate the first day of training.

"Magic holds tremendous power—it is a beacon of supreme wisdom and the search for the truths of this world," said Professor Darwin. "Yet you dullards think of magic as nothing but an invitation to a job, a stepping stone to your own success, a certificate of self-expression that sets you apart from others, or even simply a strong weapon for your personal use. How truly unimaginative and shallow. Your naive complacency created by these times of relative peace and your level of stupidity makes me shudder. It is beyond deplorable. You should be ashamed."

Does this guy know how to say anything besides insults?

The students were dumbfounded at the way Darwin hurled one verbal barb after another.

"Within all great and sublime magic lurks the inescapable reality of the danger and darkness in its very nature," the professor continued. "Mages are drawn to each other by a fateful attraction. Thus, as long as mages exist, struggles between them are inevitable. History has proven this time and time again. Hence, my class teaches how one may control that very struggle between mages. And by mastering these magical struggles, we may come closer to learning certain truths. So now, you dullards—fight."

""""Huh?"""""

The students were taken aback by Darwin's sudden declaration.

"What are you gaping for, idiots? I'm telling you to immediately go at each other in magical combat. Use all the weak and pathetic magic you fools have learned so far to its greatest extent. No need to hold back."

"Uh, okay, but…you haven't taught us anything about how to use magic in battles yet…"

"Do you really think you dullards, as you are now, would be able to comprehend the theories of magic warfare if I were to teach you? Stay your arrogance. It is better to learn by doing. Right now, pick any random opponent present here and fight until one of you collapses. Once you finish that, change partners, and go again until one of you collapses. Don't worry. As long as you don't die, I'll heal your wounds. I'm just that nice of a person."

"《《《《　》》》》》"
...

"Whoever reaches five total victories *may leave.* Losers must stay. And for any of you idiot failures who are still here at the end of class, I'll give you some special training myself. I'll make you regret being born."

"《《《《　》》》》》"
...

"What are you waiting for? Oh, I see. Rather than fight your fellow classmates, you'd rather fight me? Fine, I'll humor you. Come at me, all at once."

Professor Darwin's gaze was dead serious. He raised his arm and began casting a fierce magic spell.

"Eeeeek?!"

"This is too hardcore!"

"What's this guy's probleeeeemmmm?!"

In a mad rush, the students started looking for battle partners.

————————

To put it lightly, the class was like a scene from hell.

All around the basement's magic training grounds, students were paired up and desperately fighting back and forth in magical combat.

Trying their best to utilize the spells they had only just recently learned, they put all their energy in trying to down their opponents.

Jeers. Screams. Sobbing. The sound of magic ripping through the air.

Here and there, battered, defeated students collapsed unconscious, while the winners, also looking worn-out and ragged, raised their arms in delight.

"Dammit, this class is out of control! What is the professor thinking?!" Randy yelled in frustration after finishing his first battle.

Luckily, his partner had been a beginner in magic as well, and somehow Randy had managed to win. But he was still covered in burns.

"Ugh… Ow… It hurts…"

Annie, who had also just finished her first battle, was clutching at a bruise on her leg with tears in her eyes.

She had been knocked to the ground by a spell called Air Bullet, which shot a ball of air at its target.

"Grr… I cannot comprehend this. Why would the professor do something so rash…when we have students like Annie among us who aren't suited to battle?"

Unsurprisingly, Serephina had earned a flawless victory in her first match, but she was boiling with anger over the perplexing format Darwin had forced upon them.

Uh…is it really impossible to avoid fighting, even in the world of magic…? Hrm…

Elsewhere, Rix was feeling uncertain, pondering over what Darwin had said.

No, no, that can't be right! I mean, I know mages who ended up working as magical doctors in the countryside, leading peaceful lives with their beautiful wives and kids!

This professor's way of thinking is just particularly extreme, right?! Probably! Yeah!

That aside, he needed to deal with the current situation somehow.

Pretty soon, he was going to have to take on his first battle. Darwin was watching him.

Rix started looking around for a partner, when…

"I've been waiting for this moment, Rix."

…Alfred appeared in front of him, wearing a confident expression.

"Finally, it's time to make the difference between us clear," he told Rix. "*A swordsman can never win against a mage.* It's time for you to learn the real meaning of that phrase."

"Alfred…"

"It's all right, go ahead…you can use that sword of yours as much as you like. Even if it's a real blade, a thing like that is nothing more than a tree branch against a mage. You'll accept my challenge, won't you? You won't be running away from this opportunity, right? Right, Rix?"

Alfred, seemingly already confident in his ability to win this fight, was staring silently at Rix.

This was part of a class assignment in the first place. Rix had to battle someone.

It looked like there was no avoiding this conflict with Alfred.

"Understood. Let's do this."

Rix accepted. Then—

"—?!"

—suddenly, as if he had just noticed something, he broke into a run.

"Come here, Rix. A match just finished, so there's a spot open— Gwaaaaaaah?!"

He sprinted at Alfred and knocked him over, sending Alfred flying in the opposite direction.

"Wh-what on earth?!"

"H-hey! What are you doing?!"

"Rix?!"

Serephina, Randy, and Annie hurried after Rix to see what was going on.

He was headed toward a crowd—and within that crowd, a gruesome scene was playing out.

"Gya-ha-ha-ha-ha-ha! Hey, Shino! Is that all you've got?!"

"Urgh… Urk… U-ugh…"

There, covered in burns and bruises, a pitiful sight to behold…was the White Class's notorious loner: Shino.

And standing in front of her, with a huge smile, was a large male student.

It was the Red Class's Gordan Grolyle...the same delinquent student who had caused trouble with Shino and Rix during the entrance ceremony.

He must have challenged Shino to a match, even though she was still powerless with her Sphere unopened.

"Hey, c'mon! What's wrong, scholarship student?!" Gordon taunted.

"A-aaaaaaaaahhhhhh?!"

He summoned bright lightning around his arm and mercilessly swung it at Shino.

The lightning flew in an arc and hit Shino, enveloping her whole body in its ferocious electric current. Shino screamed in pain.

"A-ah...guh..."

Shino slumped toward the ground where she stood. She looked like she was about to lose consciousness.

"Oh, not so fast!" said Gordon.

With another swing of his arm, Shino stopped on a dime before she could collapse. And then, as if held up by some invisible force, Shino's body was limply brought back to standing and unnaturally held upright.

It was likely some kind of telekinetic spell.

Gordon must have used magic to keep her conscious, because she came to again and moaned in agony.

"...Agh...ugh..."

"C'mon! It's too early to go night night... Hyah!"

Whump!

Gordon threw a strong punch into Shino's stomach while she remained suspended in midair.

"Guh?! Augh?!"

Unable to stop him, Shino trembled, and her eyes opened wide.

The fight was already over. It was clear as day who had won.

Shino wasn't able to use magic. This wasn't even a fair fight to begin with.

Yet Gordon wasn't done. He showed no signs of ceasing his relentless pummeling.

But the most incomprehensible part of the whole situation…

"…"

…was that the instructor in charge, Darwin, wasn't doing anything to halt this absurd match.

He just stared from afar with his cold gaze, saying nothing to Gordon.

"U-um…Gordon?"

"Uh… Don't you think this is a bit much…?"

And yet even Gordon's cronies were taken aback and starting to voice their concerns.

"Huh? What are you guys saying? She still hasn't *collapsed*, right?" said Gordon.

With a look of delight, he went up to Shino's suspended body and wrapped his arm around her shoulders.

"That was what Professor Darwin said, yeah? 'Fight until one of you collapses'? I'm merely following his instructions as best I can. Of course, it is starting to pain me to see her like this…but she just won't seem to quit. Little Miss Shino doesn't seem to want to give up the fight yet! I'm only doing this because I have to. I'm a hardworking model student, y'know?"

"Y-yeah, I guess so… Ah-ha-ha…"

"You are pretty hardworking, Gordon…"

His cronies couldn't deny him.

Gordon was apparently the reigning tyrant in his grade. The Red Class students tried to avoid getting involved with him as much as possible and turned a blind eye to his actions.

Gordon went up to the lifeless, limp Shino, grabbed her jaw, and lifted it with a jerk. He licked his lips like a predator with its prey captured before it.

"Well then, Shino," he said. "You and I are fighting on even terms here...but I think it's about time we settled the match. So like I've been saying, if you just say those words for me, I'll end the battle right here and now. Well?"

"Urk! I t-told you already...! Do whatever...you want...!"

Shino coughed up blood and managed to spit out a response.

"If you want me so badly...! Just do...whatever you want...! Make me your woman...or your slave... Whatever... Urgh! I don't care...! I don't have...any reason...to live— Urgh?!"

Gordon buried his powerful fist in Shino's stomach before she could finish.

"No. That isn't what I want to hear. You're only stating the obvious," he told her. "What I want to hear you say is... 'I will withdraw from the academy.'"

"...!"

Shino's gaze wavered slightly.

"'Cause y'know, you're causing trouble for me, too... If Gordan Grolyle's woman is just some incompetent failure of a student who can't open her Sphere, then how does that make me look? It's bad for my reputation. It'd make the whole Grolyle family look bad. So if you withdraw from the academy, you won't be a student anymore, and it won't be a problem, right? Then you'll just be some woman I'm keeping around for fun. Gya-ha-ha-ha-ha!"

Gordon's wildly self-centered logic was enough to make those watching sick to their stomachs.

"Gya-ha-ha-ha-ha! You should be honored! This shows how much I like you, doesn't it? If nothing else, you've got good looks! Gya-ha-ha-ha-ha!"

"Ugh... Ah..."

"Besides, what's the big deal? Who cares if you quit the academy?

You're useless if you can't open your Sphere anyway! There's no point in staying for no good reason! Your life'll be much more meaningful if you just throw this all away and devote your heart and body to me! Right?!"

"I—I..."

Trembling, Shino began to speak.

"..."

But then she stayed silent and dropped her gaze.

"Oh? Not giving up yet? You're still going to face me, Shino?" Gordon asked. "You've got grit, I'll give you that! In that case, I'll have to fight with all I've got, too!"

Gordon summoned another lightning bolt and pushed his arm against Shino.

"Aaaaaaaaaaaaaahhhh!!"

Immediately, Shino's screams, like the sound of tearing fabric, and the crash of the lightning rang out in harmony.

"That bastard...!"

"I can't watch this anymore!"

Randy and Serephina were losing their tempers.

"Professor! Professor Darwin!"

Sobbing, Annie ran up to their instructor, who was standing nonchalantly at a slight distance, and clung to him.

"Please stop him! This is too much!" she begged.

But Darwin simply shoved her away in irritation.

"From what I can tell...those two still haven't settled the battle," he said coldly.

"Settled?! But it's been clear for ages now...!"

"I said to battle *until one collapses*. I said what I said, and that's the required condition for the battle to end. A rule is a rule, no exceptions. And Shino Whytenight still has not collapsed."

"B-but...! Gordon is holding Shino up with some kind of spell...!" Annie stammered. "It's not fair! It's horrible! Don't you feel sorry for her?!"

"As I said. You all are ignorant fools. You still fail to understand the dark and terrifying side of magic."

Annie trembled under Darwin's icy gaze.

"The art of magic is not the dreamy little fairy tale you fools think it is," he proclaimed. "The history of mages is stained in blood and plagued by war. There's no place for the ethics, morals, and mercy of the common masses in magic. 'If thou seekest to achieve thy desires, thou must feed the desires of others into the kiln.' The power to push through and have your own way is everything. Do you understand? As long as you are a mage, someday, without fail, there will come a time when you cannot avoid a battle. And when that time comes, your opponent will use any and all means at their disposal to force their own way upon you. Against such an opponent, will you persuade them with mercy and morals? Will you speak of justice? If so, you should give up being a mage here and now. You'd be better off.

"Know this. Based on the rules of these training grounds, Gordon Grolyle has done nothing wrong. If anyone is wrong, it's Shino Whytenight, clinging to this academy and taking on this battle despite her utter powerlessness."

"?!"

Annie froze in shock, devastated. She was unable to accept a single word Darwin had said.

And yet...she felt the weight of those words as well as a sense of defeat.

"Ha! Professor, your logic is full of crap!"

"Indeed! I won't allow this to go on any longer!"

Randy and Serephina were ready to join in the fight. They began charging toward Gordon...

...but before they could reach him, a flash of light streamed past them and headed straight for Gordon.

"What's this?" Gordon said.

Without even looking, he snatched up the light in his fingertips.

The source of the light—was actually a throwing knife.

*   *   *

"That's enough, Gorgan."

It was Rix. Rix had thrown a knife at him.

Randy and Serephina were dumbfounded. Rix pushed them aside and approached Gordon.

"Huh? Are you messing with me? My name's *Gordon*."

"Oh, it is? Gor-whatever? Unfortunately, I can't even remember my multiplication tables."

Gordon's expression flared with dangerous rage.

The students around them began to murmur.

"…Rix…?"

Shino, her consciousness wavering, noticed Rix and moaned his name.

Ignoring everything else around them, Gordon and Rix glared at each other, face-to-face.

There was a considerable height difference between them, with Gordon looking down on Rix.

"Oh yeah. There's another piece of trash besides Shino who hasn't opened their Sphere, isn't there? Hey, trash…you think you can just come and butt in on our match like this? You trying to get killed?"

"Whatever. It's time to wrap it up. There's other people waiting for their turn."

"What? Their turn?" Gordon cocked his head in confusion.

"Yeah, your next battle is with me," Rix declared. "You won't be running away, right? You wouldn't be dragging out this battle with Shino just to avoid taking me on, would you?"

"!!"

Gordon was momentarily in shock at Rix's challenging attitude.

"Gya-ha-ha-ha-ha-ha-ha-ha!"

But the next instant, he started cackling wildly.

"That reminds me, I owe you a walloping after what happened at the entrance ceremony, huh?! Fine, let's do this. I'll smash you to a pulp in front of all these people!"

As he shouted this, an overwhelming amount of mana flowed out explosively from his body.

The ominous pressure emanating from his mana and his giantlike presence set him apart from all the other students.

"Wh-what is this? There's something strange about his mana!"

"Unbelievable... This amount of mana isn't something that can be explained simply by his age or talent! There's definitely something strange going on here!"

Randy, and even Serephina, couldn't help but be stunned by Gordon's extraordinary and abnormal mana.

Then finally, Shino was released.

The power supporting her disappeared, and she began to fall, but Rix caught her in his arms and cradled her.

"...Hold on a moment." Rix brought Shino's limp body over to where his friends were.

"...A-are you really gonna do this, Rix?" Randy asked.

"Yeah, you guys take care of Shino." Rix handed Shino over to Randy and the others.

"Wait! There's something strange about him! Let me help you fight!" Serephina insisted.

"M-me too!" Randy added. "I can't just stand by and do nothing! I might get in the way, but—"

"No, you two. Professor Darwin said it has to be one-on-one. If that's the rule he made, there's no way he'll let anyone else get involved." Rix looked over at Darwin. "Leave this to me."

With that, Rix started heading toward Gordon again.

"...Don't do it."

But someone else called out to him. It was Alfred, who had come running up to him.

"I told you, didn't I? 'A swordsman can never win against a mage.' It's a hard fact."

" "
…

"On top of that, right now, Gordon…somehow looks like his mana's power exceeds some of our instructors'. If you try to fight him, and you're not even a mage, it's not going to end well."

"Hmm? Are you worried about me?"

"Wh-why should I be worried about you? I'm the one who's supposed to fight you! I just can't have this guy snatching my opponent out from under my nose!" Alfred shouted angrily as his face reddened. "But the way you are, I guess you can't see how much of a threat he is right now."

"I can kind of get it… It's just a feeling. I can feel it in my swordsman's instinct, down to my bones… Something's telling me 'Don't fight him right now.'"

"Hmph, really? Then why are you gonna fight him?"

"It's the way we did things back at my old haunts," Rix replied nonchalantly. "You have to help your comrades—it's just a rule."

"…C-comrade…? I'm…your…?" Shino whispered, looking up at Rix. But he didn't notice.

Once again, he headed for Gordon.

"All right, let's do this, Gondola."

"It's *Gordon*. Heh-heh-heh. I'm gonna kill you, Rix."

"Just to double-check—I'm a regular guy who can't use magic," Rix said, pointing to the sword at his hip, "so is it all right if I use this?"

"Yeah, do whatever you want. Some little stick like that will be about as useful as a fart against my magic," Gordon replied with a grin. "But you know…you really threw a wet blanket over my heart-pounding battle with Shino. You're gonna have to pay me back for that."

"Pay you back? What do you want me to do?"

"Oh, it's simple. We'll wager something on this battle that's equal to my losing Shino. Let's see. If you lose, you withdraw from the acad—"

Just as Gordon was about to finish, Rix cut him off.

"Understood. I wager my life on this battle."

He said something so extreme with such a casual attitude.
"...Huh? ...Wha...?"
"If I lose, you can have it. My life," said Rix. "But in return, you have to wager your life, too."
"What?! You little jerk, are you crazy...?!"
"Crazy? Isn't that what a battle is in the first place? Or do mages do things differently?"
"D-don't start acting cocky... You think you can scare me with something like that...?!"
Gordon stared Rix in the eye.
He seemed normal, neither crazed nor desperate. Nothing like that.
And he wasn't being swept up in violent emotion or cockiness, nor was he bluffing.
Rix was his normal self, just staring straight back at Gordon.
But the fact that he was acting so *normal* was what made him *terrifying*.
"You prick... Who do you think I am?!" Gordon howled in an attempt to stifle the fear welling up inside him.
He summoned lightning...and their fight to the death began.

"Diiiiiiiiiieeeeee!"

Gordon swung his hands down.
When he did, innumerable bolts of lightning started raining down over Rix's head.
His field of vision flickered and glowed white-hot. A thunderous noise rang in his ears, and a fierce electric current hailed down on him.
But...

＊　＊　＊

"…Hup!"

…at once, Rix started running toward Gordon in a flash of speed and whizzed past him.

Then, weaving his body back and forth with the slightest movements, he completely dodged the bolts of lightning as they came down around him.

Using the shortest possible route, Rix had quickly closed the distance between him and Gordon.

"Wha—?!"

Gordon's face wavered with shock.

Then Rix drew his sword and aimed for Gordon's neck.

His sword flashed with explosive speed as he unsheathed it.

With overwhelming sharpness and precision, Rix's sword was about to meet Gordon's neck…

But then—

Clank!

—Rix's sword clashed against Gordon's neck but stopped. The blade didn't pass through even a slice of flesh.

"…?!"

"Heh-heh-heh-heh… You tryin' to threaten me?!" said Gordon.

Rix showed the slightest surprise when he saw Gordon go pale and flash a vile grin.

Gordon summoned lightning again, and Rix jumped backward.

Serephina was watching this exchange and said with anguish in her voice, "This is it…! The reason why an ordinary human can never win against a mage… A mage's defense is too strong…!"

"Yeah, that's right." Alfred pushed his glasses up. "It's the basics of the basics—physical enhancement magic. Once it reaches a certain level, a mage's body is protected by a kind of mana shield, making the body basically impervious to non-magical physical attacks. In reality, there's no way to take down a mage without using magical attacks. And that's not the only advantage mages have over ordinary humans."

Just as Alfred said this—

"Graaaaaagh!"

Gordon once again started bringing down his lightning in a frenzy.

But his target was Rix, a battle-hardened mercenary.

Rix predicted the trajectory of each bolt, and with a speed almost imperceptible to the human eye, jumped back, dodged right, tumbled left, and leaped out of the way.

He kept evading each and every lightning bolt.

However, the bolts kept aiming for where Rix was about to land as they assailed him.

No, they weren't aiming for him—it was as if they knew where Rix was going to go next and had been planted there.

Then suddenly, there was a direct hit.

"Guuuuh?!"

Rix's face contorted in anguish as pain shot throughout his whole body.

"Wh-what was that just now?! Was he able to read exactly where Rix was moving? Even though he was moving so fast...?!" Randy's eyes were peeled wide in disbelief.

"That's the second major advantage mages have over ordinary humans," said Alfred. "Did you forget? Mages are omnipotent within their own Spheres."

"Oh! Th-that means..."

"Right. Mages can perfectly sense and grasp any phenomenon that occurs within the boundaries of their Spheres. No matter how inhumanly fast Rix moves, no matter how much he tries to feint, it doesn't matter. Gordon can see everything. And as long as he knows how Rix will move, there'll be plenty of ways to deal with him."

Then, before Alfred and the others…

"Man, you're a slippery little thing… Just behave for a second, will ya?"

The moment Gordon said this—
"…?!"
Rix's movement, and his speed, blatantly slowed.
Then Gordon's lightning attacked once again.
"He used a debuff…?!"
"Looks like it," Alfred remarked. "Against another mage, he wouldn't have had such an easy opening, and there's always the risk of getting countered with a curse. But if your opponent is just an ordinary human, there's no risk. He can curse Rix all he wants. That's what happens when a regular human fights within the bounds of a mage's Sphere." Alfred sniffed before continuing. "In a fight between mages, it's essentially a struggle between the bounds of each Sphere. It all comes down to whittling down the opponent's Sphere and controlling the field with your own Sphere. But if it's a regular human…a swordsman can't do that. No matter what, the swordsman has no choice but to fight unprotected in that zone of almost certain death, within the mage's Sphere. That's why it's a common saying in the magical world: 'A swordsman can never win against a mage.'"
Randy and Annie fell into a hush.
Then—

Okay. This is going to be harder than I thought…
Rix was starting to feel this keenly after fighting Gordon for real.
He understood this after barely one minute of their battle.
He knew he didn't even have a one-in-a-million chance of winning this fight.
Noticing that Rix must have finally realized this, Gordon laughed smugly.

"Do you get it now? This stark difference between us?" he asked. "When you knocked me down back at the entrance ceremony, that was nothing but a fluke. You happened to catch me off guard, and I couldn't use my physical enhancement and my Sphere in time. When I'm fighting for real, there's no way a piece of trash like you could ever win against me..."

Clang!

Before he knew it, Rix had disappeared from Gordon's field of vision and had sneaked up behind him.

And Rix was thrusting his sword into Gordon's back.

Gordon had no way of knowing, but this had nothing to do with Rix's speed—it was pure excellent skill. It was the ability of an assassin to strike at the gap in their target's attention.

Even though Gordon had a mage's omnipotence, and even though he had weakened Rix's body with a curse, he still wasn't able to keep up with that movement.

Gordon couldn't stop a chill from running up his spine.

While Gordon's physical enhancement magic blocked Rix's sword, and the blade hadn't broken through...he could sense the frightening precision of the position of Rix's sword. He was aiming for his heart.

Whether it was his neck or his heart, Rix was clearly aiming to kill Gordon.

And Gordon sensed absolutely no hesitation from Rix.

Without his physical enhancement magic, or if Rix's sword had been enchanted by someone, Gordon would already be dead twice over.

"Wh-why, youuuuuuuuu!!"

Filled with humiliation and anger, Gordon summoned another lightning spell.

The sound rattled the atmosphere. The whirling light assaulted their vision.

This time, there was no dodging it.

"Gwah?!"

Rix took a direct hit of the lightning and was sent flying.

It was a decisive hit.

To a human like Rix, this was the end of being able to put up a good fight against Gordon.

"Trying to make a fool out of meeeeeeee?! I'll make you wish you'd never been boooooooorn!"

This time, Gordon not only cast his lightning but explosive flames, storms of ice, and cutting winds, too—he showered Rix with all sorts of magical attacks.

It was enough to make the spectators reconsider how bad Gordon's torture of Shino had been.

Rix was being destroyed—burned, scorched, slashed, beaten, and ground to a pulp.

The gruesome scene unfolding before them rendered everyone watching speechless.

———

Ah… This feeling… I'm gonna die…, Rix thought in a daze as the terrible violence and pain of Gordon's magic racked his entire body.

He could tell that he was coming exceedingly close to death.

This sensation of impending death, which he had become so familiar with since his childhood. Now it was right in front of him.

Ahh… This really brings me back…to those days…in the Forest of Endyard…

The lightning assaulted Rix over and over again.

I can hear it now…that old song…

The flames badly burned his body.

Oh crap… I can see it… I see it again… That light at the tip of the sword…

The cutting winds sliced him to bits.

Red voids of blood bloomed over and over on his skin.

No...that light... *I never wanted...to see it again...but...*

But still, somehow, Rix wanted to live.

He wanted to live as a human.

However—when he saw *that light*—he could feel himself losing his humanity all over again.

He wanted to live as a human. But he was so far from anything human that when he tried to live as one, he became a self-contradiction.

"Rix! Dammit! Hold it together, Riiiiiiiiiiix!"

"Stop! Please, that's enough!"

"Rix! You've done your best! But please, you can stop now! Allow me to help—!"

He heard his friends' voices growing increasingly distant—friends so great they were wasted on someone like him, who didn't have any right to be alive.

Being able to meet them had made coming to this academy worth it.

To be able to live out a happy life, in a world free from fighting... I guess I knew it was never possible for me from the start... But I wish I could stay with them just a little longer... So...

And thus, Rix decided to give up just a little bit of his humanity.

"Man...I'm impressed you could stay standing even after all that."

Gordon's snide voice echoed across the training grounds.

He had momentarily stayed his attacks, and standing before him was Rix, at death's door.

Rix looked terrible. It was a wonder that he was even still alive. He had stabbed his sword into the ground and was using it to support his body.

"So? Do you finally understand it, the difference between you and me? Get on your hands and knees and promise to be my slave for the rest of your life, and maybe I'll forgive you. What do you think?" Gordon asked Rix.

"…ne…and…"

"Hmm?" He noticed that Rix, in a daze, was whispering something. "Huh? Hey… What the heck are you saying…?"

"…One fruit, red and ripe…"

Gordon strained his ears.

"…Two fruits, round and sweet…"

Rix was singing to himself.

"…Three fruits, small in size…"

It sounded like something a mother would sing to get a baby to sleep…a lullaby.

The lyrics weren't particularly special. It was like countless other lullabies sung around the world.

But…what was it about it?

"Ugh, ah… A-aaaaaaaaaah…?!"

As soon as he heard those lines, Gordon's whole body was seized by fear.

His heightened senses as a mage and his omnipotent Sphere understood in an instant: He had to kill Rix right away.

If he didn't, Gordon himself would die.

Huh…? Kill…? I—I…have to kill a person…? Gordon thought.

But the idea of this burden, too heavy to bear, made Gordon hesitate.

If he killed a person, he certainly wouldn't be able to stay at the academy, and it could cause problems within his noble family.

Of course, he had lived alongside violence up until now, but never more than a "half killing."

So he hesitated. He couldn't help it.

And that one moment of hesitation…was fatal.

"…In the woods we loved, the Forest of Endyard…"

At that moment, Rix, who had looked completely defeated, pulled his sword out of the ground…slowly raised it…and began to move, like some kind of puppet or machine.

Something about his form, his existence, was purely terrifying. Terrifying. *Terrifying.*

"Ugh, ah, waaaaaaaaaaaaaaaAAAAAAAAAAAAAAAAAAHHHH HHHH?!"

In an attempt to blast Rix away, Gordon charged up a lightning attack with both hands, even more powerful than ever before—but it was already too late.

"…The fox cub cries…"

In an instant, Rix disappeared from Gordon's vision.

But Gordon thought he saw something… A *light* at the tip of Rix's sword.

———

"Wh-what…just happened…?"

All the students who had been watching the fight between Rix and Gordon were dumbfounded.

Before them they saw Rix, with his sword unsheathed, and Gordon frozen in a daze, standing back-to-back.

No one had been able to see what exactly had happened.

All they had seen was that *light*…or at least they thought they had.

"Y-you… What…did you do…?" Gordon stammered.

Trembling, he began to turn back toward Rix…

"Gwaaahhhhhhhh?!"

…but instead coughed up blood.

They could now see that Gordon's body had been slashed cleanly, from his left shoulder down to his right hip.

It was unfathomable. An ordinary human, with nothing but one attack from a sword, had broken through Gordon's physical enhancement barrier created by his Sphere.

"Gyaaaaaaaaah?! It hurts! It huuuuuuuuuuuuuurts! A-are you serious?! S-someone help meeeeeeee!"

Having narrowly escaped a mortal wound, Gordon cried out and fell floundering to the ground.

He had completely lost his concentration and soundness of mind. There was no way for his Sphere nor his physical enhancement magic to retain its shape.

In this state, Gordon was no more than an ordinary human.

Faced with this unbelievable scene playing out in front of them, not a single soul moved.

Except one.

"…"

It was Rix.

He walked silently over to Gordon and stood by his side.

Rix's eyes were like bottomless voids.

"Eek?!" This had Gordon terrified. "I—I got it! I understand! I—I lost! I won't mess with Shino anymore! I'll get on my hands and knees and apologize! So—so please, just…!"

Heedless to Gordon's pleas, Rix silently raised his sword.

He turned it around, passed it to his other hand, and aimed the tip toward Gordon's head.

Gordon began trembling even harder.

"...Wh-wha...? Hey, you're kidding... You're joking, right...?! You weren't serious...when you said we would wager our lives on this fight...right?! Right?!"

Gordon looked up at Rix.

Rix's eyes were completely devoid of emotion. They were endlessly dark and empty. He was like an automaton executing orders.

It was already clear what Rix was about to do.

"N-nooooooooo! Mamaaaaaaaaaa!!" Gordon screamed, panicking.

Rix aimed for Gordon's head and brought down his sword in a flash.

As he did, everyone instinctively covered their eyes in anticipation of the terrible scene they expected to witness.

Slash!

However, Rix brought down his sword not on Gordon's head but the spot on the ground right next to it.

"Juuust kiddiiiiing!" Rix teased. "As if I'd ever do something like that. This is just a practice match in the middle of class, y'know? I'm joking around, obviously. So, uh, anyway...Shino, could you let go of me?"

Shino had wrapped her arms around him from behind and was clinging to him.

It was almost as if she had been desperately trying to stop Rix from going off to some faraway place.

Shino, having registered that Rix was just joking around like always, let out the faintest sigh of relief and released him.

"...Hmph."

Then, with a sniff, she turned away from him.

With Shino still in the corner of his eye, Rix started teasing Gordon.

"Well, did I scare you? Scared you good, right? Right?"

Gordon didn't answer. He was splayed out unconscious on the ground with his eyes rolled back, foaming at the mouth.

"Uh-oh, maybe I went a little too far...? Sorry." Rix scratched his head awkwardly upon realizing he might have done something wrong.

"Phew... So it was just a joke... For a second there, I thought you were serious..."

"Y-you really made me nervous..."

"Thank goodness..."

Randy, Serephina, and Annie, who had been watching with bated breath, heaved sighs of relief.

The tension building up among the other students also began to dissipate.

"But...why could Rix's attack suddenly pass through Gordon's defense?" Randy wondered.

"Well, perhaps Gordon was starting to lose his concentration during the match, and that created an opening in his physical enhancement spell. I can't think of any other explanation."

"Hmph, so he was saved by the other guy being a foolish bastard. What dumb luck."

Serephina and Alfred offered their theories.

For the most part, they seemed to agree on how Rix had been able to achieve such a miraculous comeback victory.

As Rix watched their discussion out of the corner of his eye...

"But really...I would have never imagined you'd go so far as to cling to me like that to try to stop me."

...he tried talking to Shino, who had her back to him.

"Wait, did I really look that out of control? I'm a little shocked, to be honest," he added.

"......Whatever."

Shino falteringly tried to get up and leave, but she was still badly hurt. She instead fell flat onto the ground.

"Whoa?! Shino?! Are you all right?!"

Rix went to run over to her, but...

"Uh, actually...I don't feel so good, either..."

...he, too, collapsed on the spot.

"Wh-whaaaaaat?! Riiiiiiiiiix!!" Randy hollered.

"Annie! Heal him! Do it now!" Serephina ordered.

"O-okay!"

The students fell into a frenzy once again.

"Hey," said Darwin. "I'll have you know...you're still in class. Hurry up and move on to your next match, you fools."

"Whaaaaat?! Even after all that?!"

"Seriously, what's up with the teachers at this school?!"

Darwin's unfazed demeanor was enough to put the students at their wits' end.

Chapter 7
Two of a Kind

In the infirmary situated in one corner of the school building...

There were several white beds lined up in a row, and a large arched lattice window facing outward offered a view of a lake surrounded by mountains and forests.

The walls were lined with medicine shelves, which were filled with various kinds of magic potions that appeared to be for medicinal use.

Two figures lay upon neighboring beds.

"..."

"..."

Rix and Shino.

Thanks to the healing magic and secret tinctures administered by the academy physician, Lucia Healius, the pair's wounds were recovering perfectly. Not a single mark remained on their bodies.

However, apparently it was better to recover their lost strength naturally over time, so they had been told to rest in the infirmary for a while.

And at that moment, they were the only two people there.

Of course, Gordon had been there, too, but as soon as his treatment was complete, Lucia and Darwin had for some reason whisked him away.

Since their consciousnesses had still been fuzzy when it had happened, Rix and Shino weren't sure about the circumstances or details surrounding the event. And they weren't really interested, either.

"But man, Professor Lucia is incredible. With all those injuries, I really thought it was going to be impossible for me to recover... Not to mention she's beautiful and has a great figure."

Feeling awkward in the silence, Rix decided to try to chat with Shino while using his arm as a pillow.

He honestly wasn't expecting much of a response, but...

"...Oh? So you're into older women, are you?"

...to his surprise, Shino responded, staring blankly at the ceiling.

"Well, yeah. It's a universal truth that adolescent boys all over the world are into older, more mature women."

"Hmm. Disgusting..."

Even though Rix had succeeded in making conversation, Shino was as harsh as ever.

But her present pouty air was a departure from her usual demeanor.

Thinking this whole situation was pretty dull, Rix stifled a yawn.

Then suddenly, Shino slowly sat up in bed and started talking to him.

"...I've seen your true nature."

"Huh? Where'd that come from?"

Rix was surprised by the sudden, strange topic, but Shino went on anyway.

"You are...a *puppet* trying its hardest to act *human*."

"!"

For a second, Rix didn't know how to respond, but then he decided to take it like a joke.

"...Ha-ha-ha. What makes you say that? Where'd you get that from?"

"A feeling. And I'm usually right."

"*Bzzzt*, sorry, but you're wrong about that one! Man, I'm getting hungry..."

Rix did his best to dodge the subject.

"If, at that time…" But Shino didn't back down. "At the end of your battle with Gordon—that moment. If I hadn't stopped you…would you really have stayed your sword?"

"…"

Rix didn't know how he should respond.

"Back in the day…I went through a lot of stuff," he whispered with a sigh once he had finally collected his thoughts. "Are you gonna tell everyone that I'm actually some messed-up, crazy psycho?"

"Whatever. I don't care. I just found it strange."

"Found what strange?"

"To be frank, you're not the kind of person who can live in the world of daylight. You're meant to live in a blood-soaked world of darkness. You'll never be able to escape that curse of blood and death and war… And I think you yourself know this."

"…"

"And yet…you're trying. Trying your hardest to make a place for yourself in this world of daylight. You may know it's futile deep down, but you're desperately fighting to act human anyway. After watching you for the past month…I can tell."

"Huh? You mean you've been watching me this whole time? N-no way—does that mean you *like* me?!"

"Idiot. Drop dead."

Those were just about tied for the sharpest, most painful words Shino had ever said to him.

Rix nearly fainted from the emotional pain, but Shino kept going.

"So why do you keep up such a futile effort? What meaning does it have?"

Rix interlaced his hands behind his head, looked up at the ceiling, and calmly replied, "Hmm? Is it so bad to make an effort at something that might be futile? Does there have to be some meaning to it?"

"!"

This time, it was Shino who was lost for words.

Rix shot her a grin and went on. "I just want to be happy. I want to become a mage, get a job that lets me put those bloody battles behind me, find myself a cute wife, and lead a fun and peaceful life. Then in the end, I wanna die lying in bed surrounded by my grandchildren."

"..."

"That I exist in this world, in this place, at this time, is a miracle. So what's wrong with wanting to take full advantage of that miracle and do what I want with it? If it turns out to be futile...then I'll cross that bridge when I come to it."

"..."

"And anyway...miracles might actually happen, right? They happen all the time in fairy tales...you know, like a puppet gets kissed by a girl and turns into a real human. If I do my best, I might finally get my one chance to turn everything around, yeah?"

Shino didn't react in the slightest.

The room was overcome with a strange silence.

Rix started thinking, *Hmm, so even that fell flat?* Then he timidly looked over at Shino's profile.

That was when he heard a *drip, drip...* Drops of water were hitting the blanket.

"..."

For some reason, Shino was crying quietly.

"Wha—?! H-hey, Shino...what's wrong?! Did I say something weird?!"

Shino answered Rix's question with one of her own. "Hey...can I ask you one thing? Just...hypothetically... Just if...after all..."

"Y-yeah...?"

"If there was someone who didn't have the right to exist in this world... A heinous criminal who had no right to be happy..."

"I'm not sure I understand what you're getting at, but is that person supposed to be you?"

"Read the room, you idiot!" Shino yelled, in tears.

"Sorryyy!" Rix shrank back.

"Is it okay even for a human like that...to be happy? For them to want to become happy?"

"Of course it is," Rix answered simply as Shino rubbed her tears away.

"..."

"Sure, there are people who deserve to die no matter what, but... still, wanting or aiming for happiness should be each person's individual freedom, shouldn't it? And if it really shouldn't be allowed after all, then sooner or later this world would find a way to prevent that person from being happy, through fair reason and justice. I guess my case is similar. That's why...I'm prepared for whatever happens."

"Then...doesn't that mean it's futile and meaningless in the end...?"

"Maybe. But as long as I'm having fun in the moment, I'm fine with that. Life is a miracle. It'd be a waste to not enjoy it to its fullest."

With that, Shino went silent for a while.

"...Pfft...ha-ha-ha...ah-ha-ha..."

Then after some time, her shoulders started to shake as she laughed through her tears.

It was a sight Rix would have never expected from Shino's usual expressionless, straight face.

"...Shino?"

"Heh-heh... What are you going on about? Wow, that's hilarious. How foolish. You...really are...just like *him*..."

"'Him'? ...Who, your ex-boyfriend?"

"Ex-boyfriend?! I'm a virgin, I'll have you know!!"

"Sh-Shino?! Wait—what are you talking about?!"

"Huh?! Look what you made me say, you idiooooot!!"

"But I didn't do anything!"

Shino threw a pillow at Rix's face with all her strength.

Then—

"Heeey, are you alive in there, Rix?"

*   *   *

—the door to the infirmary opened, and in came Randy, Annie, and Serephina, their new robes torn to shreds.

"Man...Darwin is seriously the worst...! I swear I'll punch that guy at least once before I graduate...!"

"Hmph... And I'll help you! Let justice be done to that fiend...!"

Randy and Serephina looked pretty angry.

"...Did something happen?" Rix asked.

"Ah-ha-ha... That Professor Darwin! Once some of the students had four victories and were about to get their fifth and be able to leave, Darwin himself challenged them to a match...," said Annie.

"What?! Then it's impossible to win!"

"Yeah. After that, everyone was passing out...and not a single person was able to get their five wins and leave..."

"What the...?"

Rix could easily imagine Darwin making up some excuse like "I never said I wouldn't participate in the matches myself, did I?"

"So in the end, the professor ended up telling us we were all complete failures...and he decided to take us all on at once in a magical battle, professor vs. students," Annie explained. "Of course, he beat the tar out of us."

"It's too immature, even for a total jerk like him!"

"Argh, it really makes me so angryyyyy!"

Randy and Serephina's rage was showing no signs of cooling off.

"Actually, it's pretty amazing that we even made it out of that fight alive...," Randy mused.

"I think I saw the ghost of my grandfather, telling me to turn away from the light..."

But the next moment, the two turned pale and began shaking in fear once they remembered what had happened.

It seemed like they had been quite traumatized by the experience.

"But...I'm so glad you're okay, Rix," said Annie. "You too, Shino."

"Yeah, sorry for making you guys worry."

" … "

Rix scratched at his cheek awkwardly as Shino cast her eyes down without a word.

Then Annie took Rix's hand in hers and began to speak, like she was pleading with him.

"Annie?"

"That last moment of your fight with Gordon…I felt like…you were about to go somewhere far away…"

Annie seemed to have picked up on whatever had happened within Rix in her own way.

With his hand in hers, she stared straight into his eyes.

"Please don't scare us like that ever again. Promise me."

"…Okay, I promise. I'm really sorry."

Rix stared back at Annie and nodded quietly.

And as they gazed at each other…

"That reminds me—Rix just told me that he prefers older women."

For some reason, Shino coldly stated this before turning the other way and covering herself with her blanket.

"Hey, why did you have to expose me like that, and why now of all times?"

"…Hmph."

"What?! Is that true, Rix? Do you really like older women…?"

"Don't you go along with it, too, Annie!" Rix's cheek started twitching.

"Come on, guys! The only way to shake off this bad mood is to go do something fun!" said Randy. "Hey, Rix! This weekend, let's all go to Campbell Street and blow off some steam!"

"That's exactly right! What we desperately need right now is some entertainment!" agreed Serephina.

Looking around at his friends, Rix couldn't help but break into an awkward grin.

———

Some days later, after school, at the magic ceremonial ground known as the Stone Circle...Rix and Shino were working on opening their Spheres under the supervision of Professor Anna, as usual.

"U-um...? Shino? Uh, you...," the professor stammered.

"...!!"

It was as if all her struggles up until now had been nothing whatsoever. Shino's Sphere had been easily unlocked.

Shino appeared surprised as she gazed at the five-meter-wide Sphere around her.

"Congratulations, Shino! Oh, thank goodness!" Professor Anna was clapping joyfully. "I'm just so glad you were finally able to open your Sphere!"

"You finally did it?! That's great, Shino!"

Rix took the dumbfounded Shino's hands in his and rejoiced like it had been his own accomplishment.

"Although...I wonder why you were suddenly able to open your Sphere like that," he mused.

"...I'm not sure..."

As the two of them cocked their heads in confusion, Professor Anna cheerfully offered an explanation.

"Actually, unlocking your Sphere has much to do with your own state of mind, your heart...mental factors, that is. Say, Shino. Might you have had any big changes in your mindset lately?"

Shino glanced over at Rix. Not a moment later, she looked away and muttered, "Hmm...I have no idea."

"Aw, really...? Hrm, I was really hoping you had some kind of hint that might help me, too..." Rix scratched his head, sounding disappointed. "In any case, congrats, Shino! This means you won't have to withdraw from the academy!"

"H-hmph! Shouldn't you be worrying more about yourself?!" Shino's face reddened before she turned to continue speaking to Professor

Anna. "Professor, thank you very much for your patient guidance and encouragement of someone so unskilled as I. And also...I hope you will continue to exercise the same toward this idiot. Please don't give up on him."

"Shino?"

Rix blinked in surprise at Shino's unexpected comment.

"...Huh? Oh, of course! That's right, we still have Rix's Sphere left to open, don't we...? Perhaps it was a little early to be celebrating, ha-ha-ha..." Professor Anna smiled awkwardly.

Shino bowed to Professor Anna before turning on her heel and leaving.

As she passed Rix, she whispered to him, "...Keep trying. As hard as you can."

"!"

Rix felt his face growing warm.

Well, if even Shino's going so far as to encourage me, now I really gotta do my best!

With that renewed sense of resolve, Rix took the Fool's Elixir in his hand and downed it in one chug.

Chapter 8
An Incident on Campbell Street

"…Pardon me."

Darwin knocked on the door to the headmaster's office and entered. Inside…

"Yes! I've been waiting for you, Darwin!"

…was Headmaster Jake…

"Hey, Darwin."

…and the instructor for the physical enhancement magic class, Crawford.

The two of them were sitting on a sofa with a finely made glass coffee table between them, drinking what looked to be expensive wine.

"A glass for you?" Crawford said to Darwin.

"No, thank you. I don't drink."

"You're a drag, as usual. Ugh…what a pain…" Crawford dejectedly withdrew the wineglass. "By the way, Darwin, I heard you had your first class in your usual fashion again?"

"Hmph… I simply aim for the students to throw away their innocent fantasies regarding magic and acknowledge the terrifying, dangerous nature of it, if only a little. A little violence is the best medicine for those naive, peace-loving dullards."

"More like chemical warfare."

"Chemical warfare or not, it is essential to their education! I appreciate you taking up that dirty job every year!"

"Still, isn't there a better way to go about it? You could at least let the students know you've enforced a barrier around the training grounds in advance that prevents mortal wounds from being inflicted..."

"That's too soft. If they don't feel the true fear of death with their own bodies, the purpose of the class is completely lost."

"*Sigh*... Geez. You know, this is why the students don't like you."

Though, I suppose by the time they graduate, you manage it so most of the students don't hate you completely..., thought Crawford as he drank his wine.

But Darwin showed no sign of caring about that. "Let's get to the main topic," he said.

"Ugh... We do have to talk about that, don't we?" Crawford griped. "Gah, what a pain..."

"All right, let's get straight to it! How were the results?!" Headmaster Jake asked.

"It is just as you thought—black."

Darwin took something out of his coat pocket and placed it on the glass table.

It was a bone fragment, about the size of the tip of a pinky finger.

It had small, strange black writing on its surface, and just looking at it made one feel sick.

"Professor Lucia and I thoroughly examined Gordon," Darwin said. "And we were able to excise this—a Demon Relic."

"...So it was as we feared." Headmaster Jake nodded solemnly, his voice calmer than usual.

"Ugh, what a pain..." Crawford clicked his tongue.

"The Dusk Demon—the most powerful and evil mage in history, who two hundred years ago, in the Mythical Era, plunged the world into the depths of fear and despair," Darwin began. "A dark lord of tyranny and gluttony who destroyed everything in their power and consumed all life. And these are remains of that same dark lord's body—a Demon Relic. Any who wield it come to bear the immense magical power and profound knowledge of the Dusk Demon. However...this appears to be a third-class relic."

"You're right," said Crawford, scratching his head. "Had it been second-class or higher, the entire academy would have been blown to smithereens."

"Hmm." Headmaster Jake nodded.

"But there is no doubt that he had this relic in his possession. Gordon is one of the Faith Faction," Darwin concluded.

Headmaster Jake and Crawford felt a wave of anxiety wash over them.

The Faith Faction—the dark side of this academy.

And faith magic—a mysterious kind of magic that had been wielded by the Dusk Demon.

That magic was precisely how the Dusk Demon had become the most powerful mage in human history.

For many years, the true nature of that magic had been shrouded in mystery, but the situation had changed recently, since the remains of the Dusk Demon—the Demon Relics—were unearthed.

And now at Estoria Academy of Magic, a faction of alumni had formed that aimed to revive and master the faith magic by using the magical power and knowledge obtained by the Demon Relics.

That was the Faith Faction.

For a time, the Faction was touted at Estoria Academy of Magic as the latest cutting-edge trend, a new era for the magical world...until it came to light that those who were deeply involved in faith magic saw their minds gradually deteriorate to the point of insanity. Eventually, their destructive, ruinous thoughts made them less and less human.

Naturally, this dangerous group was immediately banned and dismantled, and many of the existing Demon Relics were collected and sealed away.

However, the faction persisted behind the scenes at Estoria Academy of Magic.

While few in number, these like-minded people huddled together in the darkness, quietly planning in secret. The existence of the Faith Faction within the academy could not be denied.

"Nonetheless...Gordon is nothing more than someone else's puppet," Darwin added. "I have searched the dullard's memory using magic, and I found that just recently, someone gave him the Demon Relic. Soon after, he began drowning in its power. But he himself wouldn't know the first thing about faith magic."

"Hmmmm? That's quite a bold move for a group that's supposed to be sworn to absolute secrecy."

"Yes, how strange! There must have been something quite important going on behind the scenes for them to see value in such an action!"

"So? Who was it who gave him the Demon Relic? And what was their goal?"

"Gordon has had his memory regarding anything about it perfectly erased," Darwin replied. "It must have been the work of whatever member of the Faith Faction he became involved with."

"How unfortunate! But it's nothing new for the Faith Faction to be hard to catch! Yet still, we cannot by any means allow the Faith Faction to exist! You all still have the Dardrick Tragedy fresh in your minds, do you not?!"

Darwin and Crawford fell into a hush.

"Recently, the Faith Faction has become active once again!" the headmaster went on. "And I believe the appearance of that all-too-unnatural sea monster that attacked the ship to Estoria carrying all those new students was also the work of the Faith Faction pulling the strings behind the scenes! You two must do your utmost to be careful as well! For the truly terrifying thing about the Faith Faction is not their immense magical power! It is rather that we have no idea *who* is part of the Faith Faction!"

With this, Headmaster Jake stood, walked over to the window, and stared out at the scenery.

"They maintain a system of extreme secrecy! Anyone at the academy could be a member...instructors, students, staff...even new students are no exception! And as long as the members all have Demon Relics, their experience as mages is irrelevant—even mages as exceptional as you two could be outdone in an instant if you let your guard down!"

"Yeah, I got it. What a pain."

"..."

"Right now, there are very few people who I can trust are not a part of the Faith Faction! You two are the prime examples! Please be careful not to be caught unawares by them! I'm counting on you—until the day we are able to eliminate the Faith Faction completely!"

With that, Jake, Crawford, and Darwin brought their secret meeting to a close.

Then, on the way back to the instructors' lodgings...

"Oh yeah, Darwin. I know it's a pain, but can I ask you something?" Crawford said.

"What is it?"

"I heard a rumor... Apparently, that Rix kid was able to cut Gordon with his sword while Gordon was strengthened by the Demon Relic. Is that true?"

"It is," Darwin answered with a disparaging snort. "Most likely, Gordon got overconfident and allowed a gap between his Sphere and his physical enhancement magic to form, and Rix exploited that weak spot. The result of inexperience. So? What about it?"

Crawford puffed at his cigarette as he walked and ruffled his own hair. "Eh, I dunno... Change of subject, but...the Dusk Demon was supposed to be the most powerful mage in the history of humankind. Right?"

"...? Yes, and?"

"Thousands of mages during the Mythical Era—people whose powers were of a totally different level than those of their modern counterparts—tried to defeat the Dusk Demon…and every one of them was easily defeated and destroyed."

"So the story goes."

"But in the end, the Dusk Demon was finally vanquished…at the hands of a certain human."

"…"

"And that human who vanquished the dark lord was, quite unexpectedly…a swordsman. The most powerful dark lord, who defeated thousands of the best mages, was finally defeated by the sword of an ordinary human, not a mage. Sounds pretty fishy, huh…?"

"And where are you going with this?"

"Oh, I dunno… It just got me thinking, you know… With that whole story about Rix…"

Trailing off on a vague note, Crawford looked toward the sky and blew a cloud of his purple tobacco smoke into the air above him.

In the western ward of Estorheim, home of the Estoria Academy of Magic…

…was the third district, more commonly known as Campbell Street.

In this student district were all kinds of shops related to magic, such as those for magic supplies and instruments, magic staffs, and magic texts; almost any item necessary for student life could be found there.

In addition, there were cafés and restaurants, bookstores, and amusement facilities, and on the weekends the district was bustling with students from the academy.

On this particular weekend, Rix and his friends were among the crowd of students who had come out to enjoy the sights of Campbell Street.

"All right—let's have a toast to our first month at the academy! Good work, everyone! Cheers!"

""""Cheers!"""""

Following Randy's lead, Rix, Annie, Serephina, and Shino raised their drinks.

Presently, the gang was at a café called the Forest Brownie.

It was basically a run-of-the-mill shop with light refreshments aimed toward student customers, but with its classic and stylish interior, it had a lovely, relaxed atmosphere.

The dishes tasted pretty good considering their low prices, and they looked good to boot, which made the shop especially popular with the female clientele.

"The pastries and the tea here are really delicious!" said Annie.

"Indeed!" Serephina chimed in. "Eating sweet foods like this is truly my idea of bliss!"

Annie was happily feasting on a mouthful of raspberry-and-cream cake, and Serephina was daintily eating a bite of apple pie. They both looked quite overjoyed.

"The sweets are good, too, but I really recommend this spaghetti and meatballs. It's seriously awesome," Randy remarked as he twirled some pasta with his fork. "Hey, Rix. What did you order?"

"Don't be too surprised when I tell you…but I got sugar cubes."

Randy peered over at Rix to see a plate piled tall with sugar cubes in front of him.

"Sorry, I'm already surprised. Of all the things, why'd you order that?"

"…Hmm? I mean, this is the most caloric thing on the menu."

Rix speared a sugar cube with his fork, brought it to his mouth, and started crunching on it.

"You've got that look on your face like 'What, isn't it obvious?'" Randy grumbled. "Argh, never mind, just eat whatever you want."

He decided to give up and focus on his spaghetti.

"Ha-ha-ha, okay, weirdo," said Rix. "By the way, Shino, how's yours? Is it good?"

Rix looked over at Shino, who was sitting next to him. She was silently working on a cream puff.

"Whatever. It's fine," she said. "Not that I really care, but why am I here anyway?"

"'Cause I invited you," Rix replied.

"Is it okay for me to be here?"

"If it wasn't, I wouldn't have invited you. Hope it wasn't too much trouble for you."

"…Not really."

Shino turned the other way. It sort of looked like her cheeks were turning red.

Rix could tell she was loosening up a bit.

"Oh, that reminds me!" he said. "I got you a present to celebrate opening your Sphere the other day. Would you be so kind as to accept it?"

"…Huh?" Shino looked at Rix, her eyes widening slightly.

Then…*rattle, rattle*…Rix piled a mountain of sugar cubes onto Shino's cream puff.

"They're really good! Eat as much as you like!"

"I should kill myself for expecting anything more from you, even for a second."

"…I thought all girls liked sweets."

"This is sweet, but it's not *sweets*! You idiot! Idiot!"

"Ow! Ow?! Don't throw sugar cubes at me! Bwaaah?!"

Randy, Serephina, and Annie stared blankly at the two of them.

"They…suddenly seem more friendly lately, don't they?" Randy commented, looking entertained.

"Hrmmm…"

"Hmph…"

But Serephina and Annie just glared at Rix and Shino. Randy noticed this and laughed as if to join in with them.

"Ha-ha, never a dull moment when Rix is around, huh?"

———————

After their little celebration at the Forest Brownie, the group wandered down Campbell Street together.

They looked around at rare magic tools, checked out the latest robe fashions and tried them on, and did some shopping at the magic supplies store.

And the five of them never ran out of academy-related topics to talk about.

That professor ticks me off, that class is absurd, that dish at the student dining hall was no good—and so on.

As they walked, they engaged in various nondescript topics as anyone their age might.

And Shino, Annie, and Serephina, being girls of the same generation in a way, had their own topics to talk about...

"Hey, Shino, check out this sapphire amulet!" said Annie. "It matches the color of your eyes! This would definitely look great on you!"

"...Y-you...you think so?"

"Yeah, let me put it on you!"

"Wai— Annie, you're too close..."

"Oooh, yes, it does indeed suit her! Annie, you have exquisite taste!" said Serephina. "Might you pick out an amulet that would suit me as well? Something ruby, ideally!"

In the corner of a magic accessories shop, the three girls were chatting happily.

While Shino didn't contribute much to the conversation, she seemed fairly pleased.

By all appearances, the three of them looked like a regular group of friends.

"Good for them," said Rix.

"Yeah," said Randy.

Their arms crossed, the two boys kept a watchful eye on the trio of girls.

After browsing for a while, all five friends decided to visit a store they'd stumbled upon called Cacus's Wand Emporium.

———————

"So this is what it's like inside this kind of shop... And they sell magic wands, huh?" Rix remarked, surveying the store's wares curiously.

The walls and display shelves were packed full of a variety of products.

Surprisingly, different from what one would assume from a shop called a wand emporium, wands weren't the only items stocked on the shelves.

There were all sorts of items—weapons like swords and spears, armor like bracers and shields, and accessories like bangles and rings. There seemed to be very few actual wands.

"In essence, a magic wand is but a magical amplifier that aids in spiritual access to one's Sphere."

Serephina picked up on Rix's confusion and took it upon herself to explain.

"It matters not what shape it is. Take my rapier, for example. This is also a magic wand," she added. "Until recently, wands came in a standard shape, and consequentially, the term *wand* now refers to any instrument that amplifies mana and facilitates magic use. These days, it's commonplace to choose a wand shape that best fits your style of magic."

"Interesting," said Rix.

"Hrm... I guess I should choose one for myself pretty soon... But I have no idea what I should use." Randy surveyed the huge variety of products and started to look lost.

Then:

"Rix, you should choose one as well," Shino urged, tugging at Rix's sleeve.

"A wand? Even though I can't use magic yet?"

"Yes. Serephina said it's supposed to assist in spiritual access to one's own Sphere, right? Then it should become easier to open your Sphere if you have one."

Shino looked over the wands lined up on the display shelves, eventually picked out one that was thirty centimeters long, and handed it to Rix.

"How about this? It's crafted from the wood of an ash tree, and its catalyst is hair from a pegasus mane. It has excellent magical conductivity, so it should be perfect for a beginner like you. I'll buy it for you as a thank-you for the other day."

Perhaps confident in her own powers of discernment, Shino looked proud of her choice of wand for Rix.

"This one's no good. It's too light. And too brittle," Rix said in total seriousness. "This thing won't last a minute if I start swinging it around."

"You won't be using it for physical attacks, you meathead!" Shino howled.

"W-wait! Wait, wait! L-let me pick out a wand for you, too, Rix!" Annie cried.

She hurriedly looked around the shop, picked out one that caught her eye, and brought it to Rix.

"I think this one will definitely suit you! You are very strong, after all!" she told him. "And look, it's an orcish two-handed greatstaff! It's heavy, it's big, and if you throw it, you could take out any enemy in one hit! It's perfect for you! On top of that, it's not too expensive, either, so I'll buy it for you!"

"Annie, no, you've got it wrong... We're not trying to choose a weapon for Rix... We're choosing a wand that will help him unlock his Sphere...," Randy reminded Annie, who was beside herself with enthusiasm.

Then:

"Wa-ha-ha-ha-ha-ha! You know nothing! Ignoramuses, the both of you! You understand absolutely nothing about Rix!"

Serephina let out a triumphant, high-pitched laugh.

"But I am different, you see?! I'm the woman who fought side by side with him against a sea monster!" she crowed. "And so, considering his fighting style, the current issue of unlocking his Sphere, and his potential for future growth and development, I have selected the most suitable wand for him! *This* is the only option for you, Rix!!"

Upon declaring this, Serephina proudly presented the wand she had selected to Rix. It was...a longsword.

The huge sword was about as long as Rix was tall. Forged with a high-grade magic metal, even the untrained eye could see it was well crafted. It had magic script engraved on the blade and a powerful enchantment applied to it.

This was clearly the work of a prolific magic swordsmith.

It was a masterpiece of high caliber, both as a weapon and as a magic wand to aid in the casting of magic.

"Wow! I like this one! With this, I could fight my way through any battlefield!"

Rix had a twinkle in his eye as he took the longsword in both hands and raised it up.

"Heh-heh-heh, I know, I know. I have a keen eye for this sort of thing." Serephina peeked over at Annie and Shino with a victorious grin.

"..."

Annie's usual cheerful smile had somehow turned a little scary.

"...!"

Shino had on a poker face as usual, but...*crack*...the ash wand in her hand had snapped.

"Well then, that's that! I'll purchase the sword for you right away and grant it to you as a gift, Rix! You may keep it as a family heirloom as a show of your thanks to me for generations to come!"

"Um... Princess Serephina?"

"Of course, if you should wish to express your debt of gratitude by serving as my vassal in the future..."

"Princess. Hey, Princess." Randy was poking Serephina's arm and shooting her an exasperated look.

"What is it, Randy? Can't you see I'm just getting to the good part—? Oh…?"

Randy silently pointed to a certain part of the sword that Rix still held in his hand.

It was the price tag: 30,000,000 est.

"Gwaaaaaaaaaaah?!"

Serephina let out a quite unladylike screech.

"Th-this is…"

"…About the same amount as the reward money for defeating a relatively high-class dragon."

"Th-that's too much…even for royalty…"

Annie, Shino, and Randy cringed.

"All right…so this thing is worth just one dragon, then?" Rix asked with a straight face.

"I don't have to tell you that what you're thinking is a bad idea, do I?"

Randy could only sigh in exasperation.

After that, the three girls continued to argue over Rix's wand, but ultimately, no one could decide who would get to choose and purchase one for him.

———

"So, Rix. You ended up choosing and buying your own wand," said Randy. "Though I guess practically speaking, it is best for you to choose your wand yourself…"

After leaving the wand shop, the group walked down the street.

Randy glanced over at Rix. "But why did you choose *that* thing?!"

"Huh?"

Rix looked quite proud of himself, carrying on his back a brand-new wand—a log.

Yes, *that* kind of log.

Thick and long. Freshly cut from a tree. Nothing more, nothing less.

"It's got heft, it's sturdy, it has good reach, and it was cheap... I thought pretty hard about it, and this is the one."

"Not sure you thought hard enough about the right things..."

"Hmm, you may be right. It's a little hard to carry, and I've gotta get used to how to swing it around..."

Rix grabbed the fat log in one hand and started slashing at the air.

"No! Regular humans don't just brandish logs like that! And why the heck was that store selling a log anyway?!" Randy was doing his best to keep up with Rix.

"Hmph... You should have just listened to me," mumbled Shino, who seemed a bit disappointed. She had also bought herself a wand—a one-handed type that was thirty centimeters long.

It was made of poplar, a material that was favored by many mages. This wand couldn't be used for physical attacks, but it was extremely portable and had excellent magical conductivity—perfect for quick spellcasting.

More than anything, it was an advantage to have one hand free. That way, she could use various other magic tools at the same time.

"Ah-ha-ha, it's too bad... I really wanted to be the one to choose Rix's wand."

Annie had also bought a wand. It was an evergreen oak staff about as long as she was tall (but was of course not as large as the one she had recommended to Rix).

Staffs had been the preferred wands of mages in the olden days, and while their rather low magical conductivity made them unsuitable for quick spellcasting, their high mana amplification made them ideal for casting powerful magic.

Staffs were suited to mages who wanted to stand still and cast their spells with both hands.

"But, Randy, what you opted for is rather curious as well," Serephina noted.

"You think so? Well, maybe…"

Randy looked at his hands.

He had gone with a pair of studded gloves that had magic circles on the back.

"I used to be into boxing. I went with these because I thought maybe I could put my boxing skills to use…"

"I think it's an excellent choice," said Serephina. "It is indeed beneficial to make use of one's own skills."

"In that case, mine must be a good choice, too!" Rix added confidently.

"Yeah, sure. If you think so, then let's go with that."

Randy was starting to get tired of making quips at Rix, who was happily swinging around his log.

And so as they pestered each other back and forth, the group made their way through the town.

"…So? Where to next?" Shino quietly asked Rix, who was walking beside her.

"Hmm? We didn't really have any plan in particular, besides just wandering around town and going in anywhere we found interesting… Everything okay?"

"It's fine." Shino averted her gaze. "I was just curious."

"…Don't tell me, are you actually having fun?"

"Whatever!" Shino snapped back.

Rix couldn't see her face since she was turning away, but he could tell her cheeks and ears were turning red.

Little by little, Rix felt like he was starting to understand her. She was actually pretty cute.

"…What are you grinning at? It's gross."

"Whateverrr?"

Rix tried to mimic one of Shino's usual responses as she glared back at him.

Their day of fun was flying by.

———————

"Aaah! What a great day!"

"No doubt about it."

While they had been enjoying themselves, the day had turned into twilight.

Walking through the town as it burned bright in the sunset, the group started on the road back to the academy.

"There really is much to do in this town," Serephina remarked. "It was impossible to see it all in one day."

"Yes, so let's come back again together sometime! Right, Shino?" said Annie.

"Huh? Oh…y-yes, sure… If it's okay for me to tag along, I mean…"

As Rix looked at the three girls walking ahead of him, Randy draped his arm over Rix's shoulders and pulled him closer.

"Hey, Rix. Tell me, who's your first choice?"

"First choice?"

"Don't play dumb." Randy let out a mischievous chuckle. "As far as I can tell, all three of them like you quite a bit. Though I don't think any of them are completely in love with you yet."

"You think so?"

"Yeah, I do. So? What about you? If you had to choose one of them, who would you pick? Come on, spill it: Who's your top pick?!"

"Hmm, lemme see… I still don't really know anything about relationships… I just always thought I wanted to have a cute wife in the future, so I guess, if I had to choose between the three of them…" Rix looked up at the sky for some time while he thought it over, then answered with a smile:

"All three!"

"Okay, even I'm surprised at that answer. That's pretty trashy." Randy was cringing.

"Huh? But a lot of the people in my parents' generation had about a dozen women around them at any given time. So I honestly figured I could at least do with three or so…"

"Honestly? I think I need to give you a crash course on modern relationships sometime soon."

"That'd be great! Frankly, I don't really know the first thing about male-female relations or love."

"Man, seriously? What kind of environment did you grow up in? Though it's almost weird to ask at this point."

"Anyway, what about you? Do you have a girl you like?"

"Heh, me? You really want to know? Heh-heh-heh…" Randy sounded like he had been dying for Rix to ask. "Actually…just recently, I met a real goddess at the academy…"

"Oh?"

"And the moment I met her, I knew—I knew I was born to meet her! She's in the third year, and her name is…"

Just as Randy was starting to passionately explain…

Crack! A sound like something breaking rang out above their heads.

"Wh-what was that?!"

Rix and Randy looked up to see a huge fissure in the sky shaped like a cross.

And out from that fissure, darkness began to spread at a tremendous rate—it quickly began to form a dome-like shape that covered the entire western ward's third district, where Rix and the others were.

Panic and confusion began spreading through the town. There was definitely something unusual going on.

"What is that? What the heck's happening…?" said Rix.

"…It's an Otherworld Barrier…!"

It was Shino who answered his question.

"Otherworld…Barrier…?"

"Yes. It's a basic faith magic spell…a barrier that blurs the boundary between the Material Plane in which we live and the Astral Plane that exists on the other side of it! We've been dragged into another dimension that projects the landscape of the Material Plane we were originally in! This place has already become part of the Neverwhere!"

"I have no idea what any of those words mean!"

"Ugh... It means this place is extremely dangerous! But we can't escape! Get it now?!"

"Got it!"

Then—

""""GROOOOOOOAAAHHHHRRR!!""""

—something strange started to appear around them—no, all over the town.

As if seeping out of the shadows, a pitch-black darkness like sticky coal tar swelled up, wriggled, and took various forms and shapes one after another.

Some appeared as four-legged beasts like wolves and horses, others as birds like crows and hawks, some as reptiles like snakes and lizards, more as insects like gigantic centipedes and spiders, and still others as sea creatures like octopuses and squid.

Their basic forms were familiar, but they were somehow distorted; their sharp fangs and claws sparkled unnaturally, with multiple eyes glowing and blazing ominously red.

And since they were made up of a black, irregular substance that seemed to absorb all light, they looked more foreign than any other monster that could be seen in this world.

"Wh-what are those things...?!" Randy yelled.

"Chaos Beasts—dwellers of the Astral Plane! Though these are low-class monsters!" Shino replied the next instant.

"GWAAAAAAAAAAAAAAHHHH!!"

*　*　*

A Chaos Beast in the form of a lion started heading right for Annie.

"Eek!"

Annie went pale and froze, unable to react.

But Rix was quicker.

"Annie!"

As usual, Rix rushed with unnatural speed into the space between Annie and the lion. And using that momentum, he slammed his log into the lion with ferocious power.

Bam! At the impact, the log instantly broke into tiny pieces.

"M-my loooooooooog!!"

"This is no time to be fooling around!"

"Dammit! My beloved log that fought by my side all this time…! I'm sorry, I wasn't skilled enough to wield you…!"

"Don't go making up memories that don't exist! Incoming!"

The lion, which had righted itself once again, was now headed for Rix.

In an instant, Rix deflected its claw attack and took out his sword. In a flash of light, he sliced the lion's neck.

Clang!

But his sword wasn't able to slice even a fraction of a centimeter into the lion.

"…?!"

"It's no use, Rix! The Chaos Beasts are from the Astral Realm! Unlike beings that exist in the Material Plane, physical attacks are meaningless against them!" Shino shouted.

She pulled out her wand and pointed it at Rix.

In that instant, Rix's sword took on a bright white light.

"In order to defeat them, we need mana—we need to use magic!"

"Thanks, Shino!"

Sensing what she meant, he slashed his sword like a bolt of lightning.

Instantly, the lion's head was sliced off and went flying, and the beast turned into a kind of black mist before disappearing completely.

Rix was strong as usual, but this was something more.

"Was that an enchantment spell...? She infused Rix's sword with mana...?"

"They're fast...!"

Annie and Serephina were dumbfounded by Shino's quick thinking and spellcasting.

All the while, the Chaos Beasts kept increasing in number.

"Everyone! We need to run!" Shino called to the others, who were still in shock. "At this rate, we'll be surrounded! We have to look for someplace safer...!"

"Y-you're right...! This is no time to be waiting around!"

This made Randy come back to his senses.

The group dashed through the town in search of safety from the Chaos Beasts that came forth at every turn.

With Rix in the lead, taking down the Chaos Beasts that appeared, the group made their way through the town.

"Tch! I never imagined this gear I bought would come in handy so quickly...!" Randy shouted. He took a fighting stance. *"Slice, sword of wind!"*

Chanting the incantation for the Wind Blade spell, Randy swung his hand clad in his new studded gloves.

Following the movement of his hand, a blade of wind flew forward and bisected a Chaos Bird that was coming at him.

"Oh, whooooaaaaa!"

Then, just as a Chaos Dog was leaping at him from the front, he landed his right fist on its snout while simultaneously chanting the incantation for Air Bullet.

"Unseen to eyes, bullet of mana!"

As soon as the impact landed, a bullet made of air flew out of Randy's fist point-blank and sent the dog flying.

Then, toward that same dog—

"Excellent work, Randy!"

Boom! A magnificent flame from the tip of Serephina's rapier hit the beast directly. It was burned away in an instant.

"Hyaaah!"

With a twirl on the spot, Serephina swung her rapier.

A red-hot flame spiraled around her and became a firestorm that surrounded her, blowing fiercely.

"Grrrrrrr?!"

"Eeeeee?!"

The multiple beasts that had been flying at Serephina from all sides were easily burned down by the overwhelming firepower.

"A-amazing... That's a princess for you...," Randy stammered.

"What, you're not too bad yourself, you know?" said Serephina. "Quite an accomplishment for your first real battle."

"Man... Really didn't expect all those idiotic fights I got into back in my hometown to come in handy like this..."

Randy wiped at the nervous sweat pouring down his body like a waterfall, while Serephina nonchalantly swept away the remnants of the flames with her rapier.

"I-I'm sorry...everyone... I know...I have to do something...to help, too, but..."

Annie, on the other hand, was squeezing her staff with both hands as if clinging to it for dear life.

Her face was pale as death, and her entire body was trembling. "I-I'm just so scared...!"

"Worry not; it is to be expected! And being a member of the nobility, it is my duty to protect the weak," said Serephina. "All you have to do is stand still and let me protect you."

"Instead, why don't you focus on healing? You're the best among us at healing magic, Annie," Randy suggested.

"O-okay…!"

She wiped the tears from her eyes and tried her hardest to keep up with the others.

"I know Rix's skill has always been inhuman, but…"

Randy looked ahead and watched as Rix swung his sword, which had been enchanted by Shino. He slashed over and over to cut down the Chaos Beasts as they came at him.

Rix was strong, especially against an opponent that wasn't a mage.

"Indeed, that is true, but…now it looks like he isn't the only one."

"Yeah."

Serephina and Randy nodded to each other and turned toward the group's rear.

There, they saw Shino, who had taken the role of rear guard—

"Hmph."

Shino swung her wand.

As she did, multiple small balls of lightning appeared around her— and the next moment, each ball emitted a bolt like a laser, in all directions.

The bolts shifted and moved freely around Shino as if by their own free will—completely cutting down all of the beasts around her through and through.

She swung her wand again.

From its tip came a fireball of tremendous heat.

As she flung it forward, the fireball produced a huge explosion. In one section of the explosion rose a huge pillar of fire, which blasted countless beasts into the sky and burned them to a crisp.

Passing the burning beasts in the air, countless birds swooped down from the sky toward Shino.

Calmly, Shino twirled her wand, kicking up a hollow tornado.

The birds were slashed into shreds.

"Graaaaaawwwwwwwhhhh!!"

Then a beast like a huge boar rushed toward her, stamping and shaking the ground as it approached.

Looking vaguely irritated, Shino whipped down her wand.

Craaaaash!

An immense force of gravity came down upon the boar's head and flattened it in an instant.

"Amazing…"

"I had no idea…Shino had that kind of power…"

The number of different spells Shino easily had at her disposal was beyond what her peers were capable of. She was clearly as strong as one of the academy's instructors, if not stronger.

She might have even been on par with Professor Arca.

Each spell Shino cast had fearsome accuracy and power.

On top of that, she was casually using high-level magic that no new student would possibly know, and all via chantless spellcasting.

Furthermore, she gave the impression that she was used to magical combat. She looked like a regular battle-hardened mage.

"Did she really only just open her Sphere…? What's going on…?" Randy wondered.

"I haven't the slightest…," said Serephina.

"Everyone! I've got this section under control!"

Then Shino caught back up with the rest of the group, having completely taken care of beasts encroaching from behind.

"…Guh… Ah…"

"Shino?! Are you all right?!"

Serephina caught Shino as she suddenly went limp and lost her balance.

"Huff…huff…huff…huff…"

Shino was panting. She looked weak and was horrifyingly cold to the touch. She had completely exhausted all of her energy, even in such a short battle.

"Shino…have you already used up all your mana…?!"

"Yes, it seems so… How unsightly of me…"

Indeed, Shino had been wielding her magic recklessly. However, it was still too soon for her to be this exhausted.

Using up her mana at this rate... Could it be that her Sphere and amount of mana haven't caught up with her knowledge of spells...? Serephina wondered.

It seemed her Sphere was still only at a beginner level, having opened just a short while ago.

Judging from her Sphere and mana alone, Serephina was at an over-whelmingly higher level than Shino.

As far as Serephina could tell, Shino's Sphere was only about five meters wide. That was normal for a beginner; ten meters would be exceptional, and twenty meters or more would be considered prodigious.

In short, Shino's Sphere was merely average. Her powers were typical of a beginner mage.

However, there was no doubt that her skill level was excellent; she was able to send her spells outside the boundaries of her Sphere, where such extreme force and attenuation began to occur.

But now was not the time to be questioning the unnatural disparity between Shino's skills and her actual power.

"Over here!"

Ahead of them, Rix had cut a bloody path through their enemies and was waving at Serephina and the others.

"Let's go, Shino," said Serephina. "Lean on my shoulder."

"...I'm sorry for the trouble."

"Just hang in there, Shino...!" said Annie.

Supported on either side by both girls, Shino staggered onward.

With Randy keeping lookout and Rix in the lead, all they could do was keep on running from the beasts that continued to appear one after another.

Chapter 9
The Dusk Demon

It seemed the Chaos Beasts were appearing within the town as well.

Naturally, since it was the weekend, many academy students were around—including upperclassmen, who were able to protect themselves and deal with the situation.

Not everyone was that capable, of course, and there were also ordinary citizens present who couldn't use magic at all.

Their screams and cries could be heard throughout town.

But Rix and the others, still budding mages, didn't have a spare moment to worry about them.

Was there anywhere within this closed barrier that was safe to begin with?

With this anxiety in their minds, they still could do nothing but keep running and searching.

While the beasts continued to appear endlessly, a feeling of despair had begun to creep over them little by little.

However, that despair was suddenly, unexpectedly blown away.

———————

Rix and company, still being chased by the beasts and barely escaping with their lives, happened upon a deserted plaza…

＊　＊　＊

"Everyone! You're all right!"

To their surprise, they came upon a woman wearing a black robe.
It was someone they recognized.

"Oh, Professor Anna?!"

"What are you doing here?!"

She was their instructor from the academy.

Upon noticing Rix and his friends, she breathed a sigh of relief. "I
had some errands to run, so I was in town today!"

"Oh... So that's why..."

All the instructors working at the academy were highly skilled
mages. Randy, too, breathed a sigh of relief.

"Right now, I'm working together with the academy's upperclassmen to rescue any new students or townspeople in need!" the professor told everyone. "So please rest assured, the situation is more under
control than it looks!"

"I—I see... That's a relief..."

"Yes... Honestly, it's been quite the ordeal..."

Annie and Serephina started to calm down.

"You five are some of the few who are left! Come, hurry this way! I've
prepared an escape path to the outside of the barrier!"

"Whoa, really?! Leave it to Professor Anna!"

"Thank you so much, Professor!"

"Heh-heh-heh! Well, everyone, it looks like we're saved! Let's go!"

Randy, Annie, and Serephina responded with cheerful expressions.
The girls were still supporting Shino; Anna beckoned them over, and
then...

Claaaang! The sound of a sword and a staff clashing rang out.

"Huh? Rix?"

"..."

Rix had aimed an attack at Anna, who was visibly surprised as she blocked Rix's sword with her staff.

For a moment, everyone was shocked at what they had just seen.

Then, eventually...

"You idiooooooot!! What the hell do you think you're doing?!"

"Wh-why would you do something so rude to Professor Anna, after she went out of her way to come and save us?! You should be ashamed, you fool!"

Unable to let this slide, Randy and Serephina started scolding him noisily.

"..."

But Rix didn't seem to care. He kept staring straight ahead at Anna between their crossed weapons, his expression unusually serious.

"Hmm...? Is there something suspicious about me?" Anna tilted her head to one side, looking confused.

"Just a feeling," Rix replied quickly. "And I'm usually right. Thanks to that, I've survived this long."

"H-hey, Rix, what do you think you're saying...? This isn't funny, man...," said Randy.

Rix ignored him and continued in a matter-of-fact tone.

"If I had to give a reason, I'd say it's because you only ever look at Shino, Professor. This whole time, ever since the beginning. That time you defended us from Darwin in the Headmaster's office, too. And during our after-class Sphere opening exercises. And now. No matter what, your eyes are only ever on Shino... You've never given me so much as a glance. I always thought it was kind of strange...so I've had my eye on you."

"..."

"So. Professor...right now, you're planning on killing everyone here except Shino, aren't you? You weren't hiding it very well...that intent, that malice. You may be a first-class mage, but you're only a second-class assassin. It's written all over your face... I know, because I grew up in that world," Rix explained with an icy glare, ignoring his friends' confusion. "I don't know a lot about magic, but…you're the instigator of this entire situation, aren't you, Professor?"

And then:

"Ah-ha-ha, oh my, Rix. Really, what are you saying?!" Anna let out a strange laugh. "…Those lines of yours…were not supposed to be in the script."

The next moment, a huge amount of the same darkness that made up the Chaos Beasts rose up around Rix and Anna like a geyser.

"Here's how the story goes," Anna began. "The caring Professor Anna, always considering the welfare of her students, rushed to her pupils with all her might in order to attempt to save those who had been too late to escape…but unfortunately, she didn't make it in time and only discovered the corpses of Rix, Randy, Annie, and Serephina.

"But mysteriously, she did not find Shino's body—she had gone missing… We can only assume she was eaten by the beasts, with nary a bone left behind as evidence. Oh, what a terrible incident indeed… Yes, that sounds about right. Now, please stick to the script, or else we're going to have some trouble, understood?"

A massive herd of beasts materialized from the overflowing darkness—and they started rushing Rix from all directions.

"Guh—?!"

Rix retreated, cutting them down with his sword from one end to the other as he fled from the dire situation.

"Wha—?! Those Chaos Beasts…"

"N-no way…"

Serephina and Annie gaped in shock.

The Chaos Beasts that had just appeared had clearly been summoned by Anna, and she was controlling them.

In short…it meant what they feared.

Just like Rix had said, Anna was the mastermind behind this entire situation.

"I…cannot afford to be run out of the academy just yet," she managed. "So—while it pains me to do so, I must erase all witnesses. I will erase all of you, except Shino. I'm very sorry, but…I cannot allow any of you to escape. Please understand."

A faint, cold smile played on her lips as she swung her staff.

A strong magic barrier emerged around the plaza, completely encircling it. She had closed off any chance of escape.

"A-are you serious…?!"

"Argh…what's going on…?!"

"It…it can't be true…!"

Randy, Serephina, and Annie couldn't hide their discomposure.

"…!"

Only Shino, looking like she had sensed something, was casting her eyes down, clenching her fists and shaking.

"Stay calm, everyone," Rix urged, cool and collected. "This is exactly the kind of time that we need to go against our assumptions. If we defeat Professor Anna here and now, there's no problem. Is there?"

He stepped out in front of the group and readied his sword once again.

"I have no idea how you think you're going to reverse this situation…but you may have a point…!" Trembling, Randy readied his fists. "I've…still got my hopes and dreams…! There's no way I'm gonna die like this!"

"Indeed! I, too, have great aspirations I have yet to accomplish!"

"M-me too… I have things I want to do in the future…and I don't want to give up yet… I can't let it all end here!"

Serephina and Annie took up their wands and faced Anna.

As they did, Professor Anna took one look at all of them.

"Goodness…what a bother. What is that? Your dreams? Your aspirations? You can only get away with that kind of excuse in a fantasy novel," she scoffed, exasperated. "Do you really think you can win against me? You little fledgling chicks? Even when I am in possession of a second-class Demon Relic?"

"…What…?"

"A Demon…what?"

Rix and Randy cocked their heads in confusion at the unfamiliar vocabulary.

"Y-you don't mean…?! Y-you…!"

Shino, who had been staying silent up until now, suddenly raised her head as her expression twisted into one of shock and despair.

Anna grinned back at her.

And then she began to chant an incantation.

"…I in the mirror see not I but thee; two sides of a coin the same, seeking truth, we fellows in name…"

In that instant, like the flip of a switch, Rix started rushing toward Anna.

"Rix?!"

He moved at incredible speed. Faster than they had ever seen him move before. So fast he gouged out the ground in his wake.

"…!"

Burning with a special kind of irritation, Rix ran at Anna, thrusting his sword toward her.

He felt it. He knew he couldn't allow her to complete that incantation.

If she did, something terrible would happen.

If she did, they would all die. There would be no way for them to win.

But a swarm of Chaos Beasts closed in and got in Rix's way. They came at him like a wave.

He slashed them down from end to end, but there were too many of them for him to break through.

As Rix fought the beasts, Anna continued her incantation.

"O faceless one, clad in white, fluttering thy wings pure and untainted, descend unto this world…"

"Serephina! You have to stop herrrrrrrr!"

*   *   *

Serephina came back to her senses with a gasp as she took up her rapier.

"Charge and trample, crimson chakram!"

Serephina, who usually cast flames with chantless spellcasting, had gone out of her way to chant an incantation.

She cast Flaming Wheel, the strongest flame spell she had learned so far.

A humongous wheel, formed by enormous heat and flames, spun and rushed toward Anna. But even that was blocked by the Chaos Beasts that kept multiplying without end.

The flaming wheel merely smashed through and burned a dozen or so of those beasts without ever reaching the professor.

"Guh?!"

And during this struggle—

"O ye who returns the earth to the void with thy flames of black."

—Anna completed her incantation.

Then the darkness around them…suddenly became deeper.

A magic circle appeared under Anna's feet, and an immense amount of mana began to flow through it.

Then the shadows beneath Anna's feet wriggled and spread—and *something* appeared out of the abyss of those shadows.

In a word…it might have been best described as an angel. It had a form like a human, robed in white, with pure white wings.

However—it was undeniably grotesque.

Where its face should be, there was an open hole. Its limbs looked inorganic, almost like a machine.

Nevertheless, it had a tremendous presence and amount of magical power.

It was an existence so hopeless and absolute that you were made to realize you were no better than an ant crawling on the ground in comparison—it was a perfect superior to human beings.

"...Ah..."

"...Uh..."

"..."

Seeing it with their own eyes, Randy, Serephina, and Annie went completely speechless and fell to their knees. All they could do was stare blankly up at the strange angel.

There was no way to win. They had completely lost the will to fight.

How in the world could they stand up to something that clearly dominated humanity?

However:

"Graaaaaaaaaahhh—!"

Rix was the only one who moved.

He broke through the crowd of beasts and faced the angel that stood in front of Anna, swinging his sword fiercely against it.

Clang!

But his blade, which Shino had strengthened with her magic, broke perfectly in two.

The next moment, the angel swiftly moved its hand; countless beams of light rained down from the heavens.

And where they landed, the earth was battered with explosions.

Rix was swallowed up in the flashes of light they caused.

He was able to barely avoid a direct hit by dodging as fast as he could—but the aftermath of the explosions knocked him back and completely blew him away.

"Riiiiiiiiiix!"

Rix's body rolled away like a kicked ball before finally stopping when it slammed into the magic barrier that enveloped the plaza.

His whole body looked burned and bloodied, with his right hand and left leg bent in the wrong directions.

No one could tell if he was dead or alive.

"Everyone...have you heard of faith magic?"

Anna, accompanied by the deformed angel, calmly spoke to the group as they trembled in fear, unable to even run to Rix's side.

She sounded as if she was giving a lecture at the academy.

"On the other side of this world...exists the Astral Realm. It is inhabited by all kinds of illusory beings...Chaos Beasts, spirits, fairies, demons," she said. "However, in the deepest, darkest layers of the Astral Realm—an area known as the Qlippoth—there are unfathomable Great Beings that go beyond our human knowledge. To define them in our own terms, I speak of gods, angels, and devils.

"By extending the bounds of your Sphere to the Qlippoth, you can connect with these Great Beings, communicate with them, and summon them back to this world as another version of yourself, using your own Sphere as a surrogate. And this is what we call faith magic. It is the most sublime magic that exists in this world, the closest to the truth, and the greatest power of all."

"I-it can't be... Professor Anna...a-are you...?!" cried Serephina.

"Yes, that's correct." Together with the angel, Anna gracefully bowed. "I am one of the high-ranking members of the Faith Faction—Anna the Fair. And I am contracted with the Fair-Faced Angel, one pillar of the high-ranking Great Beings. But no need to remember all that...aside from Shino, you four will die here today."

They felt the mana of Anna's Fair-Faced Angel swell...and even Serephina couldn't help but tremble at its overwhelming power.

Ugh, we can't win...! There's no way we can win against something like this...!

She was soon drenched in cold sweat.

"...Why...?" Randy, despite his shaking, threw out a question. "I don't care about your organization or whatever... Just, why are you so obsessed with Shino...?"

Then...

"You, do not disrespect Shino—no, Lady Shino—with such insolence."

...suddenly, Anna's tone of voice shifted, taking the group aback.

Then she again turned to Shino and bowed reverently.

"Finally... Finally, it seems you have awoken, O great leader."

"...?!"

"Huh?"

"Shino is...your leader...?"

Ignoring Serephina and the others, Anna seemed to be carried away with passion.

"We the Faith Faction have long awaited this day—eagerly anticipated this day of reckoning for an eternity!" she cried. "In order to reawaken your great Sphere, we dared to impose such mental burdens upon you as inciting a sea monster to attack your ship and instigating battles with mortal fools such as Gordon. We hope you will forgive such irreverence. However, it was all for you, our great leader's sake!"

"...Sea monster...? Gordon...? You aren't saying...that was all you...?!"

"We have already prepared everything for you, my lady. For you indeed are our one true guide. Our sublime shepherd. Our sage ruler. The leader of this world. Please, lead us where you will. Walk alongside us on the path to the ultimate truth. Lady Shino Whytenight—our emblem of truth and the great founder of faith magic. Or should I say...the Dusk Demon, Lady Shenola?!"

A wave of shock washed over them.

"Shino is...?"

"The Dusk Demon...?!"

It was a name every person in the world knew.

If they didn't learn it from their childhood nursery rhymes, they surely learned it in their history of magic class at the academy.

The name of the strongest mage in history, who ruled over the Mythical Era two thousand years ago in a reign of death and darkness.

The dark lord of tyranny and gluttony. The most heinous criminal in all of human history—the Dusk Demon.

And that same Dusk Demon…was Shino?

It was unbelievable; it had to be a lie…at least as far as her friends were concerned.

Shino closed her eyes in resignation, let out a sigh, and then spoke quietly.

"Yes. I am the Dusk Demon, Shenola…or I was."

"Was?"

"In my previous life. My current self is a reincarnation of Shenola the Dusk Demon. When I was killed by that man, I was supposed to have died completely, but it seems I've been reborn into this age. Though I have no idea why."

"Yes! The Dusk Demon's soul was miraculously reincarnated into this modern age after being so unfortunately defeated by the swordsman two thousand years ago. And so it was foretold in our sacred text, the Hael Prophecy! What divine coincidence is this? Or is it a miracle? Nay, none of these! It is inevitable! It is fate! The Dusk Demon, Lady Shenola, has risen once again to guide us in our ignorance, to reign once more at the pinnacle of this world, and to unravel the truths of the universe!

"This—this is the great will of this world! Come, Lady Shenola! Please, show us once again what lies beyond the mastery of faith magic! Guide us on our journey of exploration of the abyss!"

In front of the group, who were all still frozen in place, Anna spoke with a look of feverish glee and reached out her hand to Shino…

"Screw you."

Shino spat that response back at her.

"Lady Shenola…?"

"Faith magic? Are you stupid? Faith Faction? Give me a break. Do you have any idea just what I…what the Dusk Demon did? Have modern people…learned nothing from history? Ha… You say faith magic is the closest to the truths of the universe? That it's the greatest and most sublime power? Don't make me laugh. That's nothing…but a load of crap!"

Shino was shaking with anger.

"And I, the one who went so far as to create and practice such crap with a sense of purpose, am even more of an extraordinary load of crap! I'm a scumbag fiend, worse than a piece of garbage," she added. "What are you calling faith magic?! This idiotic, comical tap dance as you overstep the bounds of the human realm?! How many innocent people do you think I killed while I was swallowed up by that ridiculous power, swept up in the joy of destruction and carnage?! What a joke! Ah-ha-ha-ha?! You want to know what lies beyond the mastery of faith magic, you say? Here, I'll tell you! Absolutely *nothing*!

"You drown in power, become intoxicated by it, and end up doing nothing but seeking more, killing, destroying, torturing others, bringing endless carnage and tyranny—and beyond that, there's nothing! Not the friends I wanted to protect! Not the family I loved! Not my beloved hometown! Nothing! Nothing! There was nothing! Nothing…! I just…loved magic so much…!

"I only wanted to use that magic…to put smiles on the faces of the people I cared about, if even just for a short while… Among all the war and chaos…I only wanted to protect as many people as I could… That was all I wanted, and yet…! And yet…I…ugh…! *Sniff…*"

Suddenly, Shino broke down in tears.

Randy, Serephina, and Annie were lost for words.

The reality that Shino was the Dusk Demon still hadn't fully hit them, and even if it was true, they had no idea what in the world they could say in response to her inner conflict and anguish.

This was a story from long, long past, one they had only read about in their history textbooks.

But it was clear that her regret was deeper than the sea, and the guilt she felt crushed her with the weight of mountains.

And those feelings of despair, helplessness, and emptiness they caused her were her true nature.

Randy and the others could only imagine what had happened in that far distant past.

But Shino's tears and her unconcealed cries gouged deep into their souls.

"Shino…"

"…Shino…"

The idea of all the conflict and anguish she must have been through was enough to bring tears to their own eyes.

"Well, I figured you would say as much."

Anna said this matter-of-factly, even though she had been left high and dry by the others.

"You did seem strangely unmotivated all this time… We were even discussing this among the other members of the Faith Faction…," Anna remarked. "…That the Dusk Demon of this era had no desire to advance the art of faith magic anymore. That perhaps you didn't wish to steward us toward the truth, nor stand at the pinnacle of this world. But I guess it was all true. It's no wonder your Sphere wasn't open… Which makes it even more curious that your Sphere suddenly opened just recently. But I suppose that doesn't matter."

Anna shrugged.

"Faced with no other choice, we the Faith Faction have actually given up on elevating you to the position of our leader. Therefore, out of the material, astral, and aetherial aspects that make up your existence, we have decided to discard that which makes up your ego: the astral."

"…Huh?"

"Hee-hee. But rest assured—your material body will be used for new Demon Relics! And your aetherial spirit will be used as a textbook to understand the truths of faith magic! We will be sure to use you to the fullest! No, we will not simply throw away our Dusk Demon! Only, we have no use for your astral heart. That weak-willed heart of yours is worth less than garbage."

Shino could only back away, horrified.

"So I'll just go ahead and kill you now, all right? We have no use for your life, after all, as long as you leave your body and spirit behind!"

Anna turned and began to slowly walk toward Shino.

"...Ah...uh..."

Shino backed away.

Randy, Serephina, and Annie didn't move. Completely overwhelmed by Anna's presence, they were unable to lift a finger.

Shino was no different.

She knew. She knew she couldn't win against Anna as she was now.

Of course, compared to when Shino had been the Dusk Demon in her previous life—compared to Shenola—Anna's power was nothing. Her existence was like a weak, pitiful insect.

There was no one who could win against the Dusk Demon, who had been in perfect control of the Great Beings, all Seventy-Two Pillars of the Qlippoth, whose power she'd simultaneously commanded as if it was her own—no one, save for that one exception.

In terms of ability and status, there was a fundamental difference between that power and that of Anna, who now acted so proud to be contracted with the Fair-Faced Angel, one of the lowest ranked of the Seventy-Two Pillars.

But not now.

Against this iteration of Anna, Shino was less than a worm.

Through her reincarnation, Shino had lost that mighty magical power and her enormous Sphere that had been immense enough to envelop the whole world.

At present, Shino was just an average fledgling mage.

She did have the knowledge of faith magic engraved upon her spirit, which still remained, but with this body's weakened magical capabilities, it would be beyond her wildest dreams to grasp the power of even one Great Being such as the Fair-Faced Angel, much less all Seventy-Two pillars of the Qlippoth.

I always believed...it would be better if I just died, Shino thought as she drew back from Anna. *I always believed my life wasn't worth living. Even after being somehow reincarnated like this...I thought I didn't deserve to exist in this world...*

This body of mine is just too steeped in sin...

Then why hadn't she taken her own life? Why did she keep on living so comfortably?

Did she cling to this world simply out of habit?

It was because...of him... He was there...

Shino started remembering that man she was so indebted to.

But for some reason, instead of his face, she saw Rix's...and the faces of the people who accepted her as a friend—Randy, Serephina, and Annie.

"No... I don't want this...!"

Then Shino suddenly came to a realization.

"Why...? Why is it...?! I...don't want to die yet...! I know I have no right to live...! I know I'm riddled with sin...but still...!"

"Ah-ha-ha. That's too bad," said Anna. "Goodbye."

Anna, accompanied by the angel...slowly reached her hand out to the crying, trembling Shino...

"...Wait..."

But just then, Rix stood in front of Shino to cover her.

Carrying his sword, which had been broken in two, and having forcibly set his broken bones back in place, he stood wavering before her.

"R-Rix...?"

"Oh…you're still alive?" Anna said to Rix. "Quite the stubborn one, aren't you?"

Rix ignored her and spoke haltingly to Shino.

"Don't cry, Shino… Don't cry… I'll do something to stop this…"

"Do something…? How…?"

"Hey, Shino. I…really wanted to become human."

Shino blinked in surprise at the abrupt, strange change of subject.

"You told me before, right? That I was a puppet trying its hardest to act human. Well, yeah. You were right," Rix said. "I think, probably…I was *designed that way*, and *produced that way*, by those people. Some kind of killing machine that would keep killing as long as someone ordered me to… That was me. Because I was a puppet, I didn't have my own free will over any of that…until Captain Black took me in."

"…"

"And that man who took me in…said this to me: 'Then it's an order. Stop being a puppet. Have your own free will and act human. Even if you have to force it.' It's funny, isn't it? That's how I was reborn as Rix Frestat."

"…"

"But I had no idea. Even acting human as Rix Frestat, I had no idea what it meant to be human. But it seemed that humans are always trying to be happy…so I came to this academy. And here…I spent every day together with you all…and I somehow started feeling like I had started to understand it a little…what it means to be human."

"…Rix…"

"It's still only been a short while, but enjoying every day together with you all…made me feel this kind of strange, warm feeling deep in my chest…and I thought that must be being human. I'm glad that I met you all, and I think I'm doing pretty well for a puppet. I feel like I can do anything, and I will do anything, if it's for you all. And that's not acting. It's for real. So I think I may have actually become a little bit human. That's why…I have no regrets. If it's for the sake of protecting you…I'll gladly quit being human. No regrets."

"Rix... Wait, what...?! What exactly are you planning to do...?!"
Shino began to panic, but Rix put that aside.

He narrowed his eyes and whispered:

"*Set.*
"*Target: Professor Anna.*
"*Exclude others at all costs. If this condition is not met, immediately commence suicide.*
"*Loading orders.*"

At the tip of his sword...a *light* began to shine.

Chapter 10
Secret Weapon

The outskirts of Campbell Street, at the boundary of the Otherworld Barrier…

"Tch…"

Darwin, who had heard about the anomaly and rushed to the scene, was placing his hands on the barrier and deploying various spells to attempt to break through it and enter the other world.

It looked like the barrier was almost on the verge of opening, but it was still going to take some time.

"…What a fool I am."

Growing frustrated, Darwin infused more mana into his attempt.

"No need to rush, Darwin. These are the students you put through that harsh training day after day. Chaos Beasts should be no problem for them."

Standing by as support, Crawford tried to encourage Darwin.

"Hmph. But those new students are in there, too. They're still nothing but foolish, dull little chicks. And judging from the situation, a high-ranking member of the Faith Faction is definitely at work here. We don't know the reason why, but based on Gordon's memories, we were able to ascertain that the Faction member is targeting Shino Whytenight. So I have no doubt she is under attack by the Faith Faction right now. And we may already be too late… I can't believe I let this happen."

"There was no way for you to know. Against an organization like the

Faith Faction that swears by absolute secrecy, you're bound to end up fighting one step behind... And besides...maybe they'll be able to get by in there better than we expect."

"What do you mean?"

Darwin furrowed his brow at Crawford's comment.

"Rix Frestat is in the same group that requested permission to go off school grounds, with Shino Whytenight. There's a high chance he's with her."

"What does that regular human fool who can't even open his Sphere have to do with anything?"

"That may be true, but...my theory is that Rix's Sphere was already open in the first place."

"...What do you mean?" Darwin asked while he continued to work at opening the barrier.

"I mean exactly what I said. Only that means his Sphere never expanded into the outside and is perfectly contained within himself... It's closed off inside his body and completely self-contained. There are precedents, right? There have been people in history, occasionally, with unique Spheres like that."

"...You mean the Ego."

Crawford nodded. "If that's true, then so what? If the Sphere can't be extended into the outside, the person can't use magic. Then ultimately, an Ego is just a regular human. They cannot become mages."

"That's true. But unlike mages who open their senses toward the outside world, an Ego, who is perfectly self-contained in their own small world, may awaken to their own unknowable techniques. If a mage is omnipotent within the bounds of their own Sphere, an Ego specializes in omnipotence over their own body. Accordingly, they have no need for magic formulas, nor the laws nor reason of the universe, and need only manifest their inner world and mental image in order to awaken their own techniques. There were people like that in history, right? Someone who was just a regular human, not even a mage...who despite all expectations was able to defeat the strongest and most evil mage in history, the Dusk Demon, with no more than a single swing of his sword..."

"...The Dawn Swordsman."

"Yeah."

Again, Crawford nodded briefly. "Rix won against Gordon... He won against someone who he should have never been able to defeat with a sword. He cut down someone whose defenses should have been absolutely impenetrable by a sword. It may be wishful thinking...but we may be able to put just a little more faith in him."

"Hmph. Don't be ridiculous."

Just then, Darwin finally succeeded in breaking through a section of the barrier.

At last, they had a way inside.

"Let's go," Darwin urged. "We'll clean up the Chaos Beasts, then rescue the townspeople and students. Then we take care of the Faith Faction. We'll make them pay for overstepping the boundaries of the human realm. We've no need for something so trifling as wishful thinking."

"All right, all right, I got it. Ah, what a pain..."

And so Darwin and Crawford stepped foot inside the barrier.

One fruit, red and ripe.

Two fruits, round and sweet.

Three fruits, small in size.

In the woods we loved, the Forest of Endyard,

The fox cub cries.

"...What...? What am I looking at...? I...?!"

Anna was dumbfounded by the scene unfolding before her.

It was all too unbelievable.

The higher being Anna had summoned, the Fair-Faced Angel...was fighting.

The Fair-Faced Angel, which Anna had summoned using her own Sphere as a conduit, was another Anna herself.

They were inextricably linked—essentially, the angel was another of Anna's external personae. As such, Anna could will the Fair-Faced Angel to move however she wished, as if she were moving her own arms and legs, and wield the angel's immense power with ease.

She shared her five senses with the Fair-Faced Angel.

So it was a matter of course that the angel was fighting, just as Anna willed it to.

But the issue was that *it had truly become a battle.*

"..."

With Rix's astonishing speed, he brought his broken sword slashing down at the Fair-Faced Angel.

And the Fair-Faced Angel freely wielded its six spears without so much as touching them.

They swung down from above like lightning bolts, twirled in a whirlwind from side to side, and thrust up from underfoot toward the heavens in a tremendous barrage of blinding blows.

Rix dodged, repelled them with his sword, and knocked down every single one.

Then in an instant, he came within the Fair-Faced Angel's reach...

...and slashed with extreme speed.

A light welled forth from the tip of his blade.

It had a golden glow, like the color of dusk.

His speed was inhuman.

The flash of light from Rix's sword caught the angel's right arm— and slashed it open.

"Khhhhuuuuugh?!"

Just as he did, the same place on Anna's right arm that Rix had slashed on the angel was cut open and started spraying blood.

The Fair-Faced Angel, which had been summoned using faith magic, was an extension of her—a persona.

In short, it was another Anna.

Hence, there was damage feedback that reflected on the mage's own body. Any damage the Fair-Faced Angel suffered would be inflicted on Anna, too.

"None of this matters! None of it!" Anna shouted.

The Fair-Faced Angel fiercely thrust its spears toward Rix.

Rix stepped forward, deflecting the spears with his sword and closing the gap between them.

A flash of his sword, with inhuman speed.

The light, bursting forth from the tip.

Slash!

It sliced at the angel's chest—and blood gushed from Anna's own chest as well.

"Aaaaaaaaaaaaaaaaahhhh?!"

The Fair-Faced Angel, unable to bear it, swung its spears with reckless abandon.

Rix, with unparalleled accuracy, dodged the spears as he retreated.

Then, as if looking for an opening, Rix continued to move clockwise around the Fair-Faced Angel, at a speed that made it look like he was disappearing with each step he took—

"What...? What is this?!" Anna cried. "I don't care about your pathetic little sword tricks or your absurd physical abilities! But how?! How...could a mere sword...land an attack on this higher form of existence...the Great Being, my angel?!"

Yes, that was the issue at hand.

Rix's sword was just a regular blade.

The enchantment that Shino had cast on it had already faded long before.

And even if it hadn't, an enchantment using Shino's current magical abilities would have inflicted no more than a tickle on the angel.

On top of everything, Rix's sword had been broken in half. It barely had any use even as a weapon.

Yet still…

"Aaaaaaaaaaahhhh!"

The angel beat its wings and, with an explosive increase in speed, moved to attack Rix from behind.

The angel's speed was no match for a human to handle.

The angel poised its six spears to take out Rix's heart.

But in another instant, Rix disappeared from sight.

What replaced him—was the light of his sword.

Rix appeared once again behind the angel.

Swoosh!

He slashed deeply into the angel's flank.

"Guh?! Agh?!"

Anna grasped at her own flank as it was dyed crimson.

"Why…? How is it possible?! A higher being's magical defenses should be far beyond that of any physical enhancement spell or Sphere of a human mage… How can you bypass it so easily?!" she said, gasping in agony. "And…without using magic or mana… With a mere sword?! What is that *light*?! What exactly is iiiiiiiiiiiiiiit?!"

"…"

Rix did not answer.

He only silently, simply, like a single gust of wind, closed in again on the angel.

Light surged from the sword.

"AAAAAAAAAAAAAHHHHHHHHHHHH?!"

Anna screamed as the angel continued to be mercilessly torn to shreds.

* * *

"R-Rix... He's amazing..."

Randy watched in awe as Rix continued to overwhelm the angel with his attacks.

"Yeah..."

Annie looked on, too, dumbstruck, as Rix sliced the angel to pieces.

"So this is Rix's true power...! I knew I had judged him well after all...!" said Serephina. "Magnificent! Indeed, he will be an asset in my pursuit of military rule!"

Serephina was convinced of this as she watched Rix slash the angel from all directions at high speed.

Nonetheless...

"...But truly...what is this power of his...? This light...?" she wondered, gazing at the light.

That light, housed in the tip of the sword Rix wielded. It was like staring at the golden glow of dusk, alone in an empty wilderness. A golden light that dazzled the eyes...yet somehow lacked luster.

That light...

"Something feels...so fleeting...," Serephina managed. "What exactly...does this mean...? When I see that light...for some reason, I can't stop my tears from flowing..."

"I know...," said Annie. "Somehow...it feels like Rix is going to disappear..."

The two girls had tears in their eyes and were filled with uncertainty.

"...The Dawn Swordsman."

Shino had suddenly whispered something.

"Shino?"

"The only human...who was able to defeat me, as the Dusk Demon," Shino continued. "And he, too...the Dawn Swordsman...wielded that light at the tip of his sword. A light that can cut through any spell and break through any magical defense. A flash of his sword that

momentarily surpasses the speed of light. In the face of that light, all the techniques of the faith magic I had mastered and all the Great Beings, all Seventy-Two Pillars of the Qlippoth, were powerless."

The light the original Dawn Swordsman had wielded was not exactly as they saw it now.

It had been faster, stronger—a divine, dazzling, beautiful light that had given hope to all who had laid eyes on it, a light like a glaring silver dawn.

Not this…lusterless golden twilight, which made one's heart ache like one was heading into a lonely, dark night.

Perhaps it was the difference between Rix and the Dawn Swordsman in terms of swordsmanship and their inner minds.

But there was no mistake that the light Rix and the Dawn Swordsman wielded was essentially the same.

"…What…?!" said Annie.

"Th-then, what exactly is it? That light?" Serephina asked.

"…I do not know." Shino shook her head. "What I do know…is that it is not magic but the technique of a regular human. A human whose Sphere is completely closed off inside their self—an Ego. It is the result of the manifestation of that person's mental image and inner mind. And…the light does not cut; rather, it opens."

Then:

"No…more…*gaaaames*!!"

Anna screamed.

The angel had already been carved into bits—and Anna herself staggered, covered in blood.

"Faith magic is magnificent! It is the closest thing to the truth in this world—a sublime power, only granted to the chosen ones like myself!" she shrieked. "And yet! And yet! And yet! You, with that lowly sword! That joke of a weapon! With not a shred of knowledge, with no magic—with that trivial technique of yours! Do you think you can make me fall so easilyyyyyyyyyyy?!"

As if in response…

Whoosh!

…a massive amount of mana flooded forth from the angel's entire body.

It gave off a tremendously violent magical power and presence that made its previous incarnation look like a mere housefly.

"Ah-ha, ah-ha-ha-ha-ha! I've had it! I've had it!" Anna hollered. "I was holding back, trying not to get Shino caught up in this! But if you must mock our divine faith magic…! I cannot take this silently, on my pride as a mage…! I'll destroy you! I'll burn this whole village! I'll burn it all down…!"

She began to chant an incantation.

"O darkness, hearken to the end of times, deep, dark as oblivion…"

The next moment, a deep, ominous darkness started gathering above the angel's head.

"O master, have mercy on us, comfort us; give us, your lost lambs, your hand of salvation…"

The darkness was like black flames.

Flames of the Astral Realm, burning unbound by the principles of logic in the present world.

"And lo, with the sounding of the third flute, thus spoke the angel…

"In emptiness itself find salvation, the hand of salvation outstretched from the great abyss…

"Thus I, sent by our master, bring the salvation of death and silence to this world, with a gentle black fire of tranquility…

"And permit the angel don the unblemished shining black robe of flame...

"O untainted black flame, the prayers of your congregation, and deeds righteous..."

This...*this* was true faith magic.

The exercise of the knowledge of the Great Beings, and the recreation of the mysteries and myths they embodied—that was the essence of faith magic.

And it was clear to see—the angel's black flame was destruction incarnate.

Once it was unleashed, the town would be no more.

A flame of despair that wouldn't cease until all was burned to the ground—down to the root, down to the very soul.

That black orb of flame hovered above the angel's head and was growing more and more enormous.

"Y-you can't...be serious!"

"I don't think even Rix can stop that... I-is this the end for us...?!"

Randy, Serephina, and Annie trembled in fear when they saw the flames.

But it was Shino who spoke up and tried to calm them.

"It's all right, everyone. Please believe in Rix."

And then—

"DIIIIIIIEEEEEEEEEEEE!!"

—Anna released her magic.

The angel let loose the violent ball of flame.

The flames, deeper and darker than the abyss, became a torrent and rushed toward Rix.

"..."

Then he slowly readied his sword over his head.

He took one step toward the encroaching black flames.

As Shino looked on, something about this sight was somehow nostalgic.

"Back then...I had a name for that flash of light that killed me," she said. "I, the strongest and most diabolical mage in all of human history... And that secret weapon, humanity's last hope to draw a winning card that could trump me, the ultimate joker. I called it—

"—the Last Card."

The moment Shino said this, Rix stepped forward at lightning speed and swung his sword down.

And a light burst forth into the world.

The dazzling flash given off by his sword sliced the encroaching dark flame in two...

...and with it, sliced the angel as well.

"GYAAAAAAAAAAAAAAAAAAAAAAAAAHHHHHHHHHHHHH-HHHHHH!!"

The sound of Anna's shrieking.

And the angel, now vanishing.

With that, the curtain abruptly closed on the scene of the desperate battle.

———

After it was all over...

"He...did it...?" Randy whispered, but no one answered.

"...Ah...guh..."

It looked like Anna was somehow still alive. She was sprawled spread-eagle on the ground, covered in blood.

The angel, that projection of another self, was destroyed.

And there was already no doubt that it had no hope for recovery.

"…"

Rix turned toward Anna.

He stood silently, facing away from Randy and the others.

"H-hey…Rix…?" Randy managed.

Scuff…

Rix started walking toward the collapsed Anna…with his sword still at the ready.

The others shuddered in fear.

They understood exactly what Rix was about to do.

"Stopppppppp!" Shino yelled. "We have to stop him! Or else he'll never be able to come back!"

That triggered Randy, Serephina, and Annie to spring toward Rix.

"Hey! Rix, stop it! Come back to your senses! Hey!"

Randy grabbed Rix from behind.

"Rix! You saved us!" Annie cried, clinging to Rix's waist. "But you have to stop now! Come back! Please! No more of this…!"

"Rix! Stop! It's over! It's all over! There's no need for you to keep fighting! Rix! Can you hear us?!" Serephina grabbed the arm that held Rix's sword.

All three of them tried to stop him, tried to bring him back to them.

However, Rix didn't even blink.

He kept moving forward, as if he didn't have three people hanging on to him, and approached Anna. He dragged his friends along with him.

"Hey! Rix! Quit joking around! You don't need to take it this far!"

Randy tried punching him.

Annie tried casting Sleep on him.

But no matter what they did, he wouldn't stop. Rix simply kept walking toward this fatal conclusion.

"Rix!"

Shino cut in front of Rix and clung to him, propping herself against him.

Of course, Rix didn't react. It proved no obstacle, and he kept walking.

"Come on, snap out of it! Do you really want to go back to being a puppet?! I thought you wanted to become human?! Don't you want to be happy?! Well?!"

He wasn't listening. He couldn't hear her.

But Shino had a deadly premonition about what was about to happen.

If they allowed Rix to kill a person right now, he would break.

And he would never be able to become human ever again.

Because a puppet was something without its own free will, that only mechanically executed commands until completion.

This was a denial of his own humanity.

And it was, above all, proof that he truly was a puppet.

In the world of mages, where words had their own power akin to their own spirit and the contract of those words was enforceable, this was an act that could not be undone.

"Stop! Please stop! You have to stop! Stop, you idiot!"

Just then, Shino's own screams made her come back to her senses.

...What am I doing?! Just screeching like some common girl?!

Think! I'm the Dusk Demon, aren't I?!

Time was running out.

Anna was already right in front of Rix.

In just a few seconds, he would reach her—and mercilessly bring his sword down onto her head.

Kill Anna—he had to complete the order he'd given himself.

But when he did, he would never be able to return to his old self— she was dead sure of that.

In the limited time available to her, Shino tried with everything she had to think of a solution.

If you really want to save him, you have to think like a mage! Don't give up; think!

If Rix is an Ego, like that man...then it's likely he's not in control of his own closed-off Sphere!

It's the worst possible situation—even if it's opened, he hasn't realized it, and he can't control it!

So as the result of a command trigger, his self becomes submerged deep in the bottom of his Sphere, closed off to his own inner world. And he can only wield the light of his sword when he's in that puppet form, automatically executing preset commands in a kind of trance... There should be no doubt about this!

And right now, he must be deeply submerged in his Sphere—much more so than the time with Gordon.

So then how can I reach Rix and pull him back out from that deep place at the bottom of his closed Sphere? How...? How can I do it...?

Shino thought.

She thought. And thought, and thought, and thought.

And then...time so mercilessly ran out.

———————

"..."

A silence like time itself had stopped overtook the entire area.

Randy, Annie, and Serephina...

...were frozen in place, with their eyes wide.

Because Shino...had placed her lips on Rix's.

Her arms were wrapped around Rix's neck, like she was clinging to a dear lover.

She stretched up on tiptoe...and pressed her mouth deeply against Rix's.

With that, Rix stopped moving.

"...I had a secret weapon at the ready, too," said Shino.

Eventually, she slowly pushed against Rix's chest and separated from him.

"According to magic theory...your self was sinking deep to the bottom of your Sphere, which is closed within your inner world," she explained. "While your Sphere is open, it has an extremely rare and unique condition in which it is contained within your body, unable to expand into the outside world. In order to pull that self out of that sinking condition, that Ego state, I needed to break through that closed-off, self-contained state, even if only for a moment.

"If I did that, I would be able to raise you back up using my own Sphere as a medium. And the simplest way to break through that self-containment of yours…was for you to accept a part of another person into your body. And, well…so…you know? There are many methods in which to do this, but…in this situation, the fastest way was…to…"

Shino's usual straight face looked flustered as she rushed through this explanation that nobody had asked for… Then…

"…Does it have to be so complicated?" Rix whispered softly. "'The puppet got kissed by a girl, and he turned into a real human.' That's enough of an explanation for me."

Then he shyly, awkwardly scratched his head.

He had completely come back to his senses.

"Hmph. That's why you're so disgusting… Idiot." Shino crossed her arms and turned the other way.

She was her usual self again—words cold as ice and sharp as a knife.

But that pouting face of hers had taken on a reddish blush, and her eyes were filling with tears.

Then…

"Riiiiiiiiiiiiiix!"

"Rix!"

"You had us so worried!"

"Whoa?!"

…all at once, Rix's friends clung to him again.

"W-wait a sec! Don't forget I'm on the verge of death, with a bunch of extremely serious injuries— Gyaaaaaaaaaah?!"

Rix screamed as his friends jostled him.

And so the turmoil of the strange incident caused by the Faith Faction finally came to an end.

Epilogue
When Tomorrow Comes

I always loved magic.

Its power was mysterious, beautiful, and fun.

It could surprise others and make them smile. They would praise me and call me amazing. Thank me. Pat me on the head.

That's why...I loved magic. And that's why I studied magic with everything I had.

I wanted to use magic to make everyone smile.

But...the world was in an era of chaos and strife. An era when the weak were ravaged and the strong did as they pleased.

And so I fought, using the power of magic. To protect my beloved family. To protect the friends I loved. To protect my cherished hometown.

To, at the very least, bring smiles to the people around me. To protect those who would be killed simply because they were weak.

I kept on fighting, using that magic I loved so much.

And so—to protect them, to make them smile, I sought more power. More.

More and more.

In this world, you could not protect anything without power. Without it, you could not make people smile.

But I wasn't able to protect those people, and one by one, those I loved fell like sand through my fingers…and each time, I sought further power.

As I prayed that next time I would be able to protect them, I sought greater and yet greater might.

As I grew stronger, more of my loved ones were lost. So I became even stronger. But I lost them yet again.

As I wept for them, I sought further power.

I repeated this cycle over and over…

When did it begin?

The next thing I knew—once my sole mission became seeking further and greater power—I had become the Dusk Demon.

My tears had long since dried up, and my means and my ends had completely changed places.

I was intoxicated by the pleasure of gaining power, by the exaltation of reaching greater heights, and by the joy of overpowering others.

I slaughtered the weak, consumed their life force, and gained even greater power.

For that purpose, I incited more warfare, more carnage, more destruction—and once I had more power, I did it all over again.

Even after there was no one left for me to protect, no one left to make smile. Even after the homeland to which I was supposed to return had long since been destroyed.

I sought power—I killed and murdered and brutalized—destroyed everything in this world that I could.

And I was yet further empowered by the mages who, in their righteous indignation, attempted to defeat me and save this world that I had plunged into darkness. But I defeated them and consumed their power for my own.

Then one day…

…suddenly, *he* appeared before me.

"I've come to save you."

*   *   *

You? Save me? Why?

"Because you're crying. You've been crying this whole time."

I am not crying. What's wrong with you? Gross.

"And yet you are. As you kill everything, annihilate everything... you're always crying. You're not shedding tears or making a sound, but you're always shouting out, like a wailing child... 'Somebody save me!' 'Somebody stop me!' I can tell...though it's just a feeling."

Impossible. I just kill and lay waste to everything for the pleasure of slaughter and destruction.
Look at you, acting as if you know me... You're just plain disgusting. Do you want to die?

"You don't have to cry anymore. That's why...I've come to you."

That man—the Dawn Swordsman—unsheathed his sword before me.
And so to eliminate this foolish, disgusting man—a mere mortal, not even a mage—who dared challenge me, I summoned the Great Beings of the Seventy-Two Pillars.

And then—I realized.
After a struggle to the death, he defeated all the Great Beings I had called upon.
Then that man's shining sword struck me—and I knew:
Ah yes...I've truly been saved.
Finally, there is an end to this hell.
I was overcome with deep understanding.

And then—after it was all over...as I perished, he spoke to me.

* * *

"You committed sins. Sins this world will never forgive. But I have judged you. And through this punishment, your sins in this life have been vindicated. Live your next life and enjoy it. Find your own true happiness.

"How about you start over and learn that magic you love so much again from the very beginning? And this time, I'm sure you'll bring a smile to someone's face.

"It's all right. I know you can do it. I pray...that in your next life, you'll be reborn as a kind and gentle girl who can naturally reach out to others... That is my sincere hope.

"...Well, I'll be seeing you."

And that...that was my final memory of my past life as the Dusk Demon.

———————

"So, Rix! It turns out you were an Ego all along!"

Headmaster Jake's passionate shout echoed throughout his office.

"Yeah, um...so what does that mean?" Rix asked.

"It means you are the owner of an extremely rare type of Sphere, one which is opened, yet closed off," the headmaster began. "I have no doubt your existence will contribute greatly to the research and clarification of the nature of the Sphere, which is still largely unexplored! And I also hear that you can wield the same flash of light the Dawn Swordsman used, in a limited capacity! I must say, as a mage myself, my interest in you is endless! It seems the nomination by the Annals of the One-Horned Goddess was on track after all!"

"Hmph. While it vexes me, it seems the fool does have a certain magical value after all," Darwin grumbled.

"And to think he really was an Ego... The magic world'll have a field day over this," Crawford griped.

Rix tried to get the attention of the teachers, who seemed to be going off on their own conversation.

"Um, so what's gonna happen to me, after all?" he asked.

"Of course! You are too valuable to throw back out into the wild!" Headmaster Jake bellowed. "And besides, you have met the minimum requirement for enrollment in this academy, that is, to have an unlocked Sphere! Therefore, I permanently revoke the temporary suspension of your expulsion decision from the academy! Congratulations! As of this moment, you are officially a student of the Estoria Academy of Magic!"

"Tch… I still haven't agreed to that," Darwin muttered.

"Hey, Darwin. Don't be like that," said Crawford. "Thanks to Rix defeating the person behind it all, we were able to lift the Otherworld Barrier quickly, and the damage was minimal overall. Can't you give him a little credit?"

"That has nothing to do with the matter at hand… Though if that is the academy's decision, I will comply."

Rix sat there awkwardly while the teachers had this back-and-forth.

But he couldn't help but squeeze his fists from the joy he felt welling up in his chest.

"So that means…I…I can become a wizard after all?!" Rix exclaimed, looking hopeful and joyous.

And then:

"No, I believe that will be impossible!"

"Of course it's impossible, you foolish boy."

"Yeah, I don't think that's gonna happen…"

Headmaster Jake, Darwin, and Crawford responded simultaneously, and Rix's face went blank in shock.

"In the strict definition, an Ego is not a mage! They are a regular human!"

"And no matter how you look at it, an Ego will never be able to use magic," Darwin added. "In the end, they can only use techniques that may seem magical. But of course, in a battle between mages, you must accept that you are basically powerless. Especially if you don't want to have a repeat of your fight against Gordon."

"Furthermore, you have to take an exam in order to become a Rank Four Estoria Certified Mage...and I don't think there's any way you'll be able to pass," said Crawford.

Rix's mouth gaped as Jake walked over and patted him on the shoulder.

"But do not lose heart!" the headmaster urged. "The academy regards a rare existence like yours as very important! At present, your powers as an Ego are still immature, and there is a danger that your entire inner self could collapse should you use those powers care-lessly...hence we will be sure to assign an expert instructor to help you, as well as study you! We'll aim to have you using your powers as an Ego as freely as the Dawn Swordsman himself someday! So please, there is no need to be pessimistic!

"Even if you cannot become a mage, you will have a number of promising possibilities open to you in your future! That's right... For example, mercenary, career soldier, adventurer, monster hunter, bounty hunter, magic hunter... The possibilities would be endless as a career combat specialist..."

"Noooooooooooo!!"

Rix's scream of despair rang out in the headmaster's office.

———

"Well, in any case, that's great you'll be able to stay at the academy," Randy said to Rix.

On their way to their next class, Randy patted Rix on the shoulder. The boy was slouched over in a gloom.

"I'll show them... I'll definitely become a mage... I will become a mage... I *will* become a mage... I *will* become a mage...," Rix grumbled. "I'll become the best mage who can't use magic...! I will...!"

"All right, now... Let's leave thinking about the future for some other time."

"Yes, that's right!"

Randy and Serephina nodded, looking slightly stunned.

"Besides," Serephina added, "I've already lined up a perfect job for you after you graduate! You'll become my—"

"No way."

"At least let me finish what I was saying!" Serephina started tearing up.

"Ah-ha-ha, but thank goodness! It seems like we'll be able to spend our days at the academy together with Rix after all!" Annie said with a warm smile. "Let's all do our best together, Rix."

"Yeah, count me in, too."

Then...

"Hmph. You're all awfully optimistic. The way I see it, this man is nothing but trouble, through and through. He's got bad luck written all over him. Though I'm not one to talk."

Shino, who was walking at the back of the group, offered a cold remark while keeping her signature expressionless look.

Rix slowed down until he was next to her.

"That reminds me... You'll be staying at the academy, too, then?" he asked Shino.

"Yes. Do you have a problem with that?"

"No... I was just a little worried that you might quit, so it's a relief."

"...Hmph."

It had come out that Shino was the reincarnation of the Dusk Demon.

After talking it over, Rix and the others decided to hide that fact from the rest of the academy.

"For some reason, Shino was targeted by the Faith Faction."

"Maybe it was because they were after her special hidden powers that led to her being selected as a scholarship student?"

They decided to leave it at that and simply ask the academy to strengthen the security around Shino for her personal safety.

After all, the Dusk Demon, the strongest mage in history, was infamous.

There was no way to predict how the academy would react to the present Shino after finding out the truth.

Of course, Rix and the others didn't care because she was their friend, but they didn't know what the other students would think about Shino when they found out, either.

For now, it seemed the best course of action to keep it a secret.

"I guess that makes us birds of a feather—a pair of troublemakers! Let's both do our best!" Rix exclaimed.

"..."

Shino let the remark pass in silence. She didn't even bother to look at Rix.

She was cold as ever, and Rix awkwardly scratched his head as usual.

"Never try something like that ever again," Shino suddenly whispered to him.

"Shino?"

"I'm saying don't go giving me hope, then try to go off and die all on your own. Frankly, it's disgusting when a person is so obsessed with saving others but doesn't care about their own well-being. Next time you try something so gross, I'll feed you to the Great Beings."

After delivering this lecture, Shino quickly turned away. But Rix could see that her cheeks and ears were taking on a faint red blush.

"Don't worry," he said. "I'll engrave that on my disgusting heart. In the grossest way possible."

"Ugh..."

With this exchange, the group kept walking toward their destination until eventually, the bell signaling the start of the next class period tolled.

———————

Meanwhile, atop the wall surrounding the academy...

"So this is Estoria Academy of Magic, huh?"

A solitary girl stood and looked down at the castle-like school grounds.

That was suspicious in itself. Very suspicious. In every respect, she was suspicious.

Her small frame was hidden under a cloak and hood from head to toe. She had belts wrapped around her shoulders, arms, and waist, and she carried a huge battle-ax on her back.

It was like she was going out of her way to look suspicious.

She could have at least tried a little harder to hide the whole brutal killer look.

With her sharp gaze peeking out from the gap in her hood, the suspicious girl spoke again.

"Rix, my brother...I never thought you'd be so crafty as to fake your own death just to get out of the corps... 'Welcome those who come our way, but chase those who try to leave to the ends of hell'... Don't try to tell me you forgot our ironclad code." Then she said, "Brother, you know the bloody battlefield is your true calling. I'll do whatever it takes...to bring you back with me!"